Best Wishes

L. D. Griffin

Cold Mountain Hunter Volume 1

Copyright © 2004 by Lessley D. Griffin

ISBN 0-7414-2021X

Published by:

INFI∞ITY
PUBLISHING.COM

1094 New Dehaven Street
Suite 100
West Conshohocken, PA 19428-2713
Info@buybooksontheweb.com
www.buybooksontheweb.com
Toll-free (877) BUY BOOK
Local Phone (610) 941-9999
Fax (610) 941-9959

Printed in the United States of America

Printed on Recycled Paper

Published May 2004

PREFACE

The sport of hunting with dogs has excited me since I was old enough to know heads from tails. As a young lad, hardly big enough to carry a basket of kindling much less a real gun, I often found myself slipping my hand-me-down air rifle outside to enjoy pulling the rusty, worn trigger at any target such as a tin can imagining it to be a treasure for a trophy room.

Most folks these days think because everything is so modernized and complicated that roaming the woods with hunting dogs is now to be a "has been" instead of "an always will be" as my grandfather would have put it. This book conveys real hunting- trip experiences from a family tradition started by him, Elbert Griffin, and his most unique and colorful heritage of bear hunting.

Elbert Griffin was born and raised in Western North Carolina with bear stock in his veins. A person must be made of a tough quality material accompanied with plentiful wind when it comes to bear hunting and my grandpa contained a sufficient amount of both, even after I was old enough to realize it.

In the past, I've enjoyed conversing with numerous old timers concerning his extraordinary characteristics in and out of the woods. He was talented at the sport and brought his family up in the midst of it and watched many men and dogs come and go, as he hand picked his most faithful crew.

I consider myself very blessed to be a grandson of Elbert and I still carry on that old heritage of his. It's gotten tough a lot of times and my family and I have squeezed through some mighty tight places but we could never find it in ourselves to let the tradition down. Through the good and the bad, I suppose I've entered the race to witness the finish.

I often think that the sport of bear hunting with dogs is one of the most trying that a person could possibly engage themselves in but I consider the hounds as family and enjoy their rare companionship. Much like humans, each one is of a different personality that sets the stage for no dull moments.

There is no doubt that a person's feelings are essential for life itself. Writing parts of this book has brought tears to my eyes along with lots of laughs as I penned them carefully. I now realize how devoted my parents were and how diligently they tried to prepare me for life in general. I thank them from the bottom of my heart and will never be able to repay the debt that I owe.

INTRODUCTION

Heaven's blessings fell like springtime dew when God placed a country boy like me in such a place as the Cold Mountain Hills to experience life's endeavors from boyhood to manhood. My life in the Cold Mountain Territory has been among the finest and more rewarding than any person could ever have hoped for. I'm guilty and have taken for granted many times the cool evening breezes and the warm sunny mornings.

Cold Mountain Hunter emphasizes a certain year in my life that means a great deal to me as I constantly age. This book details hunting experiences of that year along with capturing precious memories of the Cold Mountain Territory and other parts of the Shining Rock Wilderness that are monumental commodities of my well being.

Some authors have written about things they have heard or maybe even read about in years gone by, but it has brought pleasure to me to write this book from incidents that the Creator has allowed me to see. Writing this book has made me realize just how lucky I am to have lived my life as a country boy.

This book also explains the geographical position of much of the Cold Mountain and Shining Rock Wilderness areas. Many creeks, coves, ridges and trails are mentioned in it also along with my personal adventures in and on each of them. It explains a positive relationship between a young man eager to roam these areas accompanied by his dogs, his friends and his family.

Many people are becoming more aware that a country life in the hills of Western North Carolina is

"Heaven on Earth." Numbers of passing-through visitors have chosen to reside in the Western North Carolina Mountains permanently. I believe that choices such as these have a profound effect on people's personalities and general attitudes. My living in Western North Carolina wasn't by choice, but I look toward the stars with a thankful heart daily.

Writing this book has brought back memories to me that no doubt has made me a better person. Take the time to read it and enjoy the information of The Pigeon River Valley and The Cold Mountain Territory.

The hunting season of 1983 that Cold Mountain Hunter depicts is long gone now but unforgettable fun was the name of the game that year coupled with the makings of some life-long friendships. I wish to remember some of its greatest adventures as we relive each one to the limit.

DEDICATION

I suppose it would only be wishful thinking for a person to have the power to turn back the pages of time. It sometimes sorrows me when I recollect good times from years past and know that some of the people involved have left me here alone.

The old saying that "every dog has his day" is no less than exact. Sadness has filled my heart on numerous occasions when I finally realized that I was only daydreaming about what seemed to be yesterday's fellowships with favorite men and dogs from long ago that meant more to me than is possible to explain.

There is one spear of hope though, for I believe in the life here after and look forward to seeing those favorites again, but for now I can only grasp tight to the experiences with them from the past. Remembering those unique happenings conveys a most clear message and convicts me from within to dedicate Cold Mountain Hunter to the memory of one old man and a dog--Henry Farmer and Sailor--to whom I salute with undivided allegiance on a regular basis.

TABLE OF CONTENTS

Cold Mountain Hunter,

Volume I

A NERVOUS TIME

As the day grew to a dim, sun-setting halt, my friend Kenneth and I found ourselves sitting on a flat rock just upstream from camp trying to catch Mountain Speckled Trout for the evening meal. It's hard to explain why we were fishing two days before hunting season was to open but I admit I was sure enough nervous and I had a good reason to be.

Being a farmer here in Western North Carolina is really a busier life than most folk might imagine it to be. A lot of times that past summer I got so far behind that I could hardly see my way clear. There didn't seem to be enough daylight hours and worrying about the three months wait until hunting season didn't help anything. I often found myself over anxious waiting for the fall season to arrive.

We had a draggy, late farming season here that year and the arrival of September found me still harvesting crops. The first week of September was a real exciting time for everyone in our hunting club I reckon but me. They were planning the annual hunting trip to the Upper Peninsula of Michigan. I was still busy with the farm and all of this planning was driving me crazy.

In the past season, our dogs hadn't performed to their full potential due to unexpected extractions of certain older dogs who would have been helpful in bringing the younger ones up to their full capabilities. Bragging rights were out of the question for our young pack and September found me worried to say the least.

Our hunting club knew that the young dogs were running track scent well but we were also aware of two definite problems beyond that. The young pack was ignorant to the fact of staying together on one scent which in turn would make them more powerful and successful as a team. Therefore, many hunting days ended with the hunter at a point of exhaustion trying to keep up with two or three dog parties instead of one group as needed.

The dogs were also inexperienced when it came down to fighting a bear. They weren't cowardly by any means but they hadn't learned to watch each other closely as to work in an in-and-out rotational sort of way. The young hounds were dumb to cutting small corners that could make themselves much more productive in the heat of a moment.

Those were the problems at hand so we in turn started trying to correct them. It was a depressing, discouraging effort no doubt. People that have chosen a career to work with children in groups of five or more can relate to the difficulties involved with training them, but being successful in training ten or twelve young canines can easily be imagined by most anyone. I wish to detail some of that year's adventures with the young pack, explaining the course in which they traveled from awful to near excellent.

It was September the fifth, and finally time for the club to roll toward the north country. I was depressed about having to stay at home but managed to keep a decent spirit and accept things the way they were as I helped the club members put the camping equipment into the trucks. I've never been hurt as bad by a hard lick from a keen switch as I was when the fleet of trucks left our driveway that bright sunny morning. I really felt bad about the situation but had fieldwork waiting me.

The outback mountain streams of Western North Carolina are some of the most beautiful in the world. Exploring their rocky banks can be most relaxing, especially with a fly rod in hand.

My father called home on the night of the tenth after the first day of hunting and I knew something was wrong when he answered my question with, "No, we didn't have any luck today." This went on for five or six more days and one evening just as I was expecting his call he and the whole club drove into the driveway. I rushed out to inquire but all of my questions were answered when I looked at my father's tired face.

Somehow, the dogs had really gotten on his bad side in ten short days. I finally got up enough courage to ask one of the club members just what had happened. The news was nothing but bad as I listened carefully. The dogs had run everything from porcupines to white-tail deer, but somehow managed to put very little heat on the bears. I didn't really know what to say and I sure didn't need to say the wrong thing at that point because after a twenty-four hour tiring ride, a fellow could have gotten a slight facial disfigurement for being too inquisitive.

The woodlands of the Upper Peninsula

In two or three days, and after much thought I decided to devote most of my spare time to working the pack non stop during the twenty days of the remaining dog training season. The training season usually opens in Western North Carolina on August fifteenth making it legal to run dogs on U.S. Forest Service Property until the closest Monday to October fifteenth but guns are not allowed. Taking bears during this period is totally against the law although the dogs can get good practice time and much needed exercise after being chained by the neck for the first eight months of the year.

The farming season was slowing considerably and that left me with a lot of time. My brother and I were determined to train those dogs like the pack we had always managed to keep. For the next few weeks, he and I kept the pack in the woods. They had shown signs of improvement and after a hard day's hunt during the last pre-season week, finally put a bear up a tree for us to see. We were gradually becoming happier with their performance in the woods and decided not to hunt them anymore before opening day of gun season.

I had been helping a friend cut firewood on the West Fork of the Pigeon River in my early morning spare time. I remembered seeing several bear tracks there a few days back. One morning, one of the club members and I went there to see if we could figure out whether this bear was just passing through occasionally or staying close by.

I'd noticed while working there that several acorns were beginning to fall but enough time had then passed to tell just how many acorns the trees had produced. In the early fall season, it is difficult to take an accurate inventory while the acorns are still on the trees. The foliage is so thick that over half of the small nuts are hidden. But, when the leaves begin to fall so do they, making them much more visible on the ground.

As good luck would have it, after a one-half mile walk we found plenty of acorns and plenty of bear tracks too. After several trips to that particular ridge tracking and observing the bear's daily use, we started to get good feelings that our inexperienced pups were somehow going to do well.

It was Saturday and being just two days from opening morning, I felt a deep set of butterflies in my stomach but sitting on a big flat rock catching pretty Mountain Speckled Trout had a way of making them flutter real easy. As Kenneth and I enjoyed catching fish we discussed our hopes of pulling it off on opening day. The young dogs needed a bear knocked out relatively quick or our season wasn't only going to be a long one, but an embarrassing one with an ending record of about zero and twenty five.

Kenneth and I hooked enough fish for the evening meal and made our way very talkatively back toward camp. I could tell that he was concerned but optimistic about the pack. He always looked on the bright side of everything and I admired him for that.

Kenneth Farmer was a fairly big man at that time and was as strong as an oxen. He was tough in the woods and I figure that being a Vietnam Veteran was responsible for most of that. His eyes are sky blue and his hair is dark. I've never known him to wear his hair any other way but crew cut. I guess his military days were responsible for that also. Kenneth still resides close by and is doing fine. He can shoot a rifle as well as ever too and our friendship will exist forever I'm sure.

It was Saturday night and the opener we had all waited for was just one day away. Dark seemed like hours but it finally fell. My dad entertained everyone around the campfire with lots of old-time stories that I have always appreciated. He could unfold them with high intensity making each and everyone that was listening pay close attention.

We had a big supper on Sunday evening and after enjoying it thoroughly, Kenneth and I decided that we should feed and water the dogs for the last time before the season was to begin. After those chores had been taken care of, we all gathered to discuss our last-minute plans. As usual, my dad had the starting list embedded in his head and felt like we were ready to deal with whatever was to come our way. One of the few older dogs we had at that time was named Sailor. He was first in line, of course, and before any further words are penned, I wish to remember how handy my father was with him.

My dad is a tough man and has surely lived up to my grandfather's All Madden Bear Team. His name is Roy L. Griffin. He is well known in most of the Western North Carolina counties for his hunting accomplishments accompanied by a string of neighboring hunter friends that seems to have no end. He's liked by many and goes out of his way to make southern hospitality top priority.

He's not a very big man and I figure that fact has worked to his advantage through his years of bear hunting. He's dark complected and at that time, his hair was as black as black could get. His eyes were of first quality too and he was physically fit.

He was hard to beat when it came to working a track with Sailor to get it ready for the pack. Several questions must be answered and answered correctly when tracking a bear to that point. Dad used Sailor to help him make sure that his decisions were correct and he had overwhelming confidence in him as his strike dog.

James K. Farmer – a life-long friend

Sailor was a Finley River Chief Walker. He had short hair and soft skin. He was black and white spotted with a red-blazed face. Sailor was extraordinarily blessed by being able to understand what a human was trying to tell him, especially my father.

He knew what a hand-held radio was for sure. When a track had been followed out of a feeding ground and on to the closest water supply, my father would pull his radio out of his hunting vest to let his partners know to bring the pack. Sailor would simply amaze a body when that happened. He would look at the small device and turn his head slightly back and forth when listening to the voice that was coming back through it.

Sailor did his job right on bears and it was then time for the young dogs to assist him by staying together from start to finish. Sailor was our only ticket for training the young pack and deep inside me, I knew that he would pull it off and sure enough he did.

All of the dogs had been named for one reason or another. I never did like to call a dog just anything that came to mind. I still remember each of them as if it was yesterday. Eight starters were chosen and everything was settled. Knowing that we would hardly sleep at all, everyone retired just after dark because the bigger percentage of the party thought that opening day was to be a long one.

Four a.m. finally came and I was so glad because I had tossed and turned almost all night. A question could be asked why we rose so early that morning but there was a distinct reason. It was close to a one-hour drive to where the hunt was to begin.

Roy L. Griffin with Sailor - A match meant to be

Dad prepared breakfast while the rest of us loaded the dogs into several pickup trucks. Last minute checks were made to see that all of their collars had correct name plates attached to them and that they were buckled tight enough to not slip but loose enough not to restrict the dog's air flow.

At last we were off. As we traveled the dirt road slowly, I wondered if the bear we had been observing so closely had moved or not during the nighttime hours. At that point, all I could do was hope. I could hardly believe it when the truck came to a stop. My energy level was strutted so to speak and I was nothing but ready for some long awaited action.

Sailor was glad to get out of the portable dog box. We knew our black friend had roamed that night because Sailor winded with his nose in all directions and then started pulling eagerly toward the cove that the bear had been using regularly. Dad was positive then by observing Sailor's actions. He left with Sailor by his side and promised us to hear from him shortly on his hand-held walkie-talkie.

The small cove that we were to hunt that day is somewhat of a tricky place. Its only legal hunting boundaries are approximately two miles long and only one mile wide. All of the other land outside of that perimeter is either a bear sanctuary or unhuntable private land.

To our surprise, my father reappeared just as we were expecting a radio transmission from him. He and Sailor had found the piping hot track alright but as we listened closely, he explained how the bear seemed to be headed in an irregular direction. It looked to him as if the bruin had lined out early in the night and in his opinion was bedded close to the sanctuary line.

Disappointment overwhelmed me and looking from a pessimistic point of view instead of an optimistic, I couldn't see any way to have good luck that day. My dad looked harshly at me and said, "Don't give up that easy. This

11

situation might not be as bad as it sounds," he calmly stated, "because I've got a plan that just might work."

When my father came up with a plan we all listened because most of the time, it was one that would work. He was and still is very good at that sort of thing and when he explained his so-called strategy, we were very attentive. My dad is a natural leader of our hunting party and each of us respect him and his thoughts highly even in the present day.

He promptly requested my brother and me to take three men with us and spread apart at one hundred yard intervals across the leading ridge line as he pointed straight up the long incline. "The bear is probably laying in the big rough just below the top of that ridge," he said, "and he will run by one of you fellows when the dogs are loosened."

We had no reason not to agree and promptly went on our way. Dad assured us that he would wait one-half hour before unleashing the dogs to give us time to be in place. Thirty minutes wasn't at all adequate but knowing how anxious my father was that morning, we felt lucky to have had that much. We were to be pushed to climb the steep mile and be in our proper places on time.

We were hunting that morning on the right prong of the West Fork of the Pigeon River above Lake Logan. Lake Logan is located about ten miles south of the small town of Canton, North Carolina, on Highway 215. The ridges and coves on the right prong of the Pigeon consist of beautiful open woods but are steep to climb as most of the hills are here in Western North Carolina.

Queens Creek was the particular cove we were to run our pack in that morning which heads up to the leading Double Spring Gap Ridge or Green Mountain Ridge. This leading ridge line divides two major watersheds of the

Western North Carolina region. The trail from Queens Creek to the Double Spring Gap is good hiking but is unfortunately a touch more than uphill all of the way.

My heart was pounding vigorously and as we tugged our bodies up the trail, some of the fellows were in worse shape than me. It's always quite difficult for a pulmonary system to work properly during the first week of hunting season and mine was struggling to say the least when my brother and I finally positioned the last man in his stand.

My brother, Mark, pulled ahead of me but stayed in sight. I noticed him motion at me with a hand signal as he passed by the location where I was to stop. When I arrived there, I leaned my body back first to a small oak tree to allow my breathing to catch up. I was the fourth man on the ridge and was glad to have made it to a halting point.

Only a few seconds later, I heard Sailor begin to open up and the rest of the pack right behind him. The adrenaline in my veins was pumping stronger than ever and the dogs sounded better every second that passed. As I listened closely for the sneaky brute to slip out by me, the dogs suddenly sounded different as if they had caught up with their prey.

Side stepping through some Mountain Ivy bushes into a small clearing, I listened again to make sure and all at once they sounded like they had treed. They were only five or six hundred yards from where they were turned loose. It's unusual for a pack to tree that quick while hunting in the mountains of Western North Carolina.

I strained my ears for a third time just to be definite about the matter and that time there was no doubt. The young pack was surely stopped and it looked as if us guys on top had put in a hard pull for nothing.

My first reaction was to stay put in case the bear jumped out of the tree but the longer I stood there, the more restless I became. It's rather exciting to get cold feet in the woods. I ran off of the steep mountainside with long leaps and found myself being whistled at in about five minutes. My brother had experienced a need to go also and by coincidence chose the same path to the dogs that I had.

We stopped momentarily and whispered very few words to keep noise levels to a minimum. We knew that any abnormal sounds would be a cause for the bear to jump. We communicated with our hands in situations such as we were caught up in and not only once in our lives had that occurred.

A few years had passed since my brother and I had taken a bear together and we were in full agreement that the present was an opportune time. We started slipping very cautiously when we were approximately seventy-five yards from the tree. We stopped for a thought to inject a live round into the chamber of our Thirty-Thirty Winchesters and we were ready for whatever was to happen next.

It was most emotional. I can't explain the feeling that comes over a person when sneaking to a roaring pack of hounds within minutes of the powder action. We both were aware of the fact that we needed to get that one down because the young pack would surely be improved by doing so.

We were almost to our destination when a rifle suddenly fired only a few feet to our left. The blast took us both by complete surprise. We had no idea that anyone could have been there in the short time it had taken us to descend the mountainside. We had thought wrong because the next thing we saw was the face of a good friend and hunting partner, Glenn Parker.

The majestic scenery that Green Mountain has to offer simply adds the final piece to a puzzle that its surroundings must contain.

Glenn and another club member, Whitey, had been first to the tree. Glenn had joked with me earlier that morning about how he planned to get a bear that day and the first glance of him revealed to me that he had made his promise valid. We soon learned though, that Glenn hadn't been responsible for the shot, but Whitey had.

After sufficient congratulations to him and after petting the hounds plenty, we slowly began to tie the dogs to small trees. They barked repeatedly until they were exhausted. We didn't try to quiet them for they had earned the right to be loud and annoying.

The entire hunting group gathered to us in a short while and we enjoyed the time thoroughly. I was beginning to take serious interest in the young pack and all of us enjoyed observing their actions there. It was evident that projected success, with a little luck just might be headed our way for the Eighty-Three hunting season.

A BAD DAY MADE GOOD

Later, the hunting party was back at camp. Supper tasted good and was fulfilling after an evening of preparing the bear carcass for the freezer. Many folks have probably never heard or even thought about bear meat being fit for human consumption. Black bear is a delicacy if it is cooked properly. As kids, my brother and I often looked forward to hearing Mom speak of a scheduled day that bear meat would be on her menu. Bear meat is a lot like beef. It's dark and very course grained. On a cold winter day, the aroma from a pressure cooker filled with bear meat can overwhelm any appetite.

A bit of bad luck was on tap for the second day of hunting season because of rainy weather and after putting the pack in dry places for the night, we went inside camp early to "pick and grin" for a while and talk about the first day's victory. I enjoyed that part of camping the most for all of the club members were like one family.

There was one fellow in the crowd that I overly admired and enjoyed being around. I often recollect many good-time thoughts of an older gentleman who was very fond of me as a young boy and as an adult also. His name was Henry Farmer.

None of us called him Henry very often because his fifty-year old nickname was "Chick." Chick was a heavy-set man with a very outgoing personality. He always smiled no matter what and I can still hear his unforgettable laugh. Chick was a most humorous type of person and could add a twist of fun to just about any situation. He always wore overalls. I never knew him to wear any other type of clothing. His hair was white and he wore a cap without fail.

Henry "Chick" Farmer
a man who devoted time for young lads such as myself, this photo
reveals his constant happiness. His smile had a way of fixing
most any situation.

Chick was about seventy years old at this time and
had belonged to our hunting club since he was big enough to
carry a gun. He was a tough one in his day and harvested
many bears but at this particular time in his life was
experiencing pulmonary problems. He wasn't able to go out
into the woods on foot but for a road and radio-man he
couldn't be beat.

There have been numerous times in my past years of
hunting that I would have walked lots of extra miles back

tracking to my vehicle if Chick hadn't been thinking ahead. He knew the woods well, and would always position himself to lend me a much needed ride.

When the batteries suddenly loose power a hand-held walkie-talkie is worthless. With no communication, situations such as that didn't excite Chick for he would simply think ahead and go to where he thought you would eventually come out of the woods. Chick was willing to do whatever he could and at anytime of the day or night. I guess that's the reason that his memory is so close to my heart today--other than him being one of the best friends I ever had. Chick has passed on to the next life now but our club will honor his memory forever.

Chick had finally given up for the day claiming that he needed rest and went off to bed. At last I figured to have had enough for one day myself and with nothing else to do I slithered into my sleeping bag. It was such a good feeling and I'll never forget how the pressure burden was lifted after the first day's victory. Now, I could finally get some honest sleep.

The second day of hunting season found me peeping out of the large camper door watching it rain like crazy. I was really looking forward to hunting but since the weather was foul, I decided that a little more sleep would be good especially at four thirty in the morning. All of us rested that day and some of us went home to make sure the women folk were all right. Hunting or no hunting, the women folk came first.

It's according to what part of this great country you were raised in as to the kind of climate your body is used to. In Western North Carolina, I reckon it's impossible for your body to get used to the climate. In the fall season it may be a thick, damp, fifteen to twenty degrees in the morning and by noon be up to sixty.

I must have gotten hot and cooled off too quickly with all of the excitement of opening day because Wednesday morning found me a bit under the weather. I had surely caught cold and it can easily be imagined how all of the hunters picked at me while making plans for the next hunt. I took their kidding as well as could be expected and everyone seemed to be ready for the second hunt of the season but me.

We were camped in a government-owned camp-ground called Sunburst. Sunburst is found on Highway 215 about twelve miles south of Canton, North Carolina, and approximately two miles above Lake Logan. Further up the West Fork of the Pigeon River, about one-half mile above camp, to a huge cove to the left called Big Rock House was where our hunting party was destined for Wednesday morning.

The Big Ben alarmed at the usual four o'clock and like always, I could smell my dad's coffee bubbling over an open fire. I remember trying to get dressed quickly that morning because my throat was sore and needed a trickle of hot coffee as fast as possible. My body ached and my feet were moving slow as I made my way outside into the heavy, cool air. After breakfast we loaded our hounds and headed up the river.

It's always made me laugh to watch the hunters move after the trucks are parked and dogs are being leashed. I reckon someone is constantly worried about getting left behind. After a few chuckles I made my way up the road to reside temporarily with my buddy Chick in his warm pickup truck.

Sunburst Campground

After several cups of hot coffee from Chick's shiny age-worn thermos, I began to stare at the CB radio under the dash hoping to hear good news from my dad soon. Even though I was sick, staying in the road not knowing what was going on with the pack was just simply not my cup of tea.

Dad finally checked in with Chick and me after what seemed to be hours and gave us some positive information. He and Sailor hadn't found a track yet but assured us that it wouldn't be long because Sailor was winding heavily straight up the big cove in front of them. He promised to call back when things became hotter. A fellow can get mighty nervous just sitting around waiting. After swapping a few lies back and forth, Chick and I suddenly received good news across the airway. The hunters had sure enough struck a bear head on and had turned all of the dogs loose.

As I've mentioned before, Chick Farmer was the best radio-man that I have ever known and I just sat over against the door amazed at how he could get dog directions and everybody's whereabouts in no time flat. Some member of the club, and I can't remember just who, told us that the dogs were crossing Fork Mountain into the Little East Fork area.

The Little East Fork of the Pigeon River is a much bigger place than even most of the native people of the Pigeon River Valley realize. It joins The West Fork of the Pigeon one-half mile below the Lake Logan dam and is geographically parallel with the West Fork also. By the way a dog would travel, it's not really that far from one fork of the Pigeon River to the other, but by vehicle it is a pretty good clip and from where we were located would have taken approximately twenty minutes.

It would be near impossible to include all of the real estate belonging to the name of the Little East Fork area of the Pigeon River into one picture. Although, this photo is one of my favorites.

Chick and I discussed whether we should start down the West Fork of the River on Highway 215 or wait a few moments to see if the pack might possibly cross back onto our side of the mountain. As a normal thing, we made the wrong decision and started down the river in the pickup. We had made it almost back to camp when my brother Mark came across the air and advised us that the dogs were crossing back.

It could be easily guessed concerning the kind of self-inflicting discipline that Chick and I were engaged in as he turned his Ford around at high speed. As the truck began to straighten up and come back to our side of the road, I keyed the microphone and tried to raise my brother Mark. He immediately answered sounding very much out of breath.

My brother Mark is relatively short with a stocky muscular build with little to no body fat. Unlike myself, he never was an over eater and made sure that his body stayed in good shape all the year through. He was and still is a fellow that absolutely graduates at the top of any hunter's class. In his younger days, he was tougher than most when it came to hustling through the woods to stay in hearing of the dogs.

At this particular time in his life, he was at a ripe old age of twenty-four and his ridge running abilities allowed him the privilege of almost staying in sight of the pack. Many times, I've stood in awe wondering how he got from one point to the next in such an unbelieving short length of time.

My brother came back to me on the radio and gave me the message that the pack was up with the bear and was holding together well. The last part of his transmission was scratchy but Chick and I did hear him say that the dogs were headed for the next cove up The West Fork called Little Rock House.

That was all of the news we needed because after hunting those woods for a lifetime, Chick and I realized what was happening. Any experienced bear hunter from this area knows that a bear, while running from dogs won't normally come back to the West Fork of the Pigeon after already topping out into The Little East Fork section. This one would either tree soon or try to cross Highway 215 into a sanctuary of safety.

Mark Ellis Griffin, a compassionate brother
and a man of his word.

Chick and I were making our way hurriedly up Highway 215 back toward the action. Seeming to be hours, but actually only minutes, we positioned the truck in a pull-off area parallel with the ridge that divides Big and Little Rock House Coves.

Getting out of the truck quietly, Chick and I immediately heard the pack coming across the big dividing ridge. They sounded to be fighting hard and were moving very slow. The dogs kept on coming across the ridge and seemed to be destined for the Little Rock House side.

Just as Chick and I decided to move further up the road, the dogs suddenly started tree barking in the head of Little Rock House Cove. As we discussed the situation at hand, my brother came across the air bearing news that he could hear the pack treed and should be to them in a matter of minutes.

Gee, the blood was pumping through my veins like wild horses running and all of a sudden I found myself feeling much better. I thought seriously about taking my rifle and starting up the rugged cove toward the distant roar, but I knew how tough the steep climb would be with the added aggravation of a head cold.

There are a few things about the hills of Western North Carolina that make them very different from any other mountains in the United States. The terrain is that of the worst ruggedness and they are steep to climb. Much of the woods are cliffy and rocky and a great portion is blessed with a good stand of saw briars.

After hearing the message from my brother that he would soon be there, Chick and I stayed put, almost wearing a hole in the pavement pacing back and forth waiting for the unique sound of a Thirty-Thirty Winchester to come echoing down the cove. I can still hear Chick saying over and over, "Come on Buddy, let's hear it, let's hear it."

Highway 215 winds gracefully up the West Fork of the Pigeon River and makes for a most enjoyable drive on any occasion.

The dogs got louder as they usually do when they sense that a human is getting close to them and Chick and I were beside ourselves. The suspense was almost too much to handle.

All at once and to our surprise, the dogs sounded to be moving again. I couldn't believe it. I knew then that we had loosed our pack onto the track of a mean and experienced bruin. Chick and I listened closely to get a sure direction and to our surprise discovered the pack to be coming unusually straight down the cove toward us. As I stepped to the edge of the road, they stopped again over halfway down the steep incline and started treeing for a second time. They were louder than ever and Chick and I were beginning to figure things out.

The young pack was working to the best of their knowledge with the help of very few veteran dogs and probably didn't know how to work ideally as a team yet, but the way they were sounding they were learning fast. At that point, I was convinced that they had the potential of being one of the best packs we had ever hunted with.

Forgetting all of my ailments, I quickly explained to Chick that as far down as the dogs had come I felt confident in trying to get to them before the guys that were coming down from the top. Grabbing my Thirty-Thirty in one hand and my hunting vest in the other, I jumped the guardrail and was on my way.

Being years older now, I often find myself day-dreaming about how I could travel through the woods then and didn't seem to ever wear completely out. As a young man, I never dreamed about the fact of how aging could have such a profound effect on a human body. I definitely hadn't given it any thought that day for I was going with a heart full of desire to get to the much deserving young pack of hounds.

After crossing The West Fork of the Pigeon, I started my incline through the beautiful open woods and was enjoying every step of it. I couldn't enjoy the open woods for long though because a short distance ahead rougher terrain was sure to come.

The best that I could figure, the dogs were treed approximately one quarter of a mile up the mountain and just to the left of a certain landmark in Little Rock House Cove that our hunting party calls, "The Big Rock." The huge rock is distinct and would stand out to anyone even if they had never been there before. It measures about twenty feet across and stands at least twelve feet high. Growing out of the top, rooted in a slender crack, is a clump of Lynn trees which makes the scene very unique.

Many folks would probably wonder how all of these so-called names could be memorized by hunters and believe me it takes many years. Our hunting club members have had good teachers down through the years such as my father, who have taken lots of time explaining to us many ridges and cove positions and were made aware of the short cuts that make hunting journeys much easier. Through time we have also learned all of the creeks and their hidden secrets.

After conquering an intense Laurel thicket laced with saw briars, I suddenly broke out into a small clearing in sight of "the Big Rock." The dogs were hammering louder by the second and my heart was sounding like a drum roll in my ears. I listened curiously while giving my pulmonary system a small break. Just as I started to move again, the pack suddenly charged very aggressively down the rugged incline and sounded to be coming straight for "the Big Rock."

My legs were like rubber bands but I made them spring hurriedly to "the Rock" and barely had enough time to climb on top of it before hearing the brush break just around the hill from me.

A live thirty-thirty round was already in the chamber and my eyes were looking down the barrel waiting for the moment that powder could burn. Then it happened. I saw the black rascal coming at full speed ahead. It looked as though the bear was going to run by "the Rock" so close as maybe to touch it. The dogs were only a few feet behind and as I took the slack out of the trigger a rifle fired under me with a blast that almost stopped my heart. For a moment, I thought my rifle had fired but after looking at the hammer on my Winchester and finding it still in the cocked position made me very confused.

He had done it again. Glenn Parker, had accessed the situation to a tee and graded the mountain perfectly. He had arrived at "the big rock" just before I had and crawled under its overhanging ledge making himself hard to see. I didn't know it was him until I heard his familiar voice as it suddenly echoed from under me with laughter. The shot was a good one for the bruin tumbled to a standstill.

Glenn still resides in the Little East Fork Community and enjoys listening to a heated-up bear race as well as ever. He and his family mean a great deal to me and I still enjoy visiting his country home in its most beautiful creek-side setting quite often.

Glenn's deep voice is one that makes a body anxious to hear his next sentence. Through the years, I've had a lot of good times in the woods with Glenn and have been privileged to call him my friend.

Laughing together, Glenn and I had very good fellowship as we waited on the rest of the hunting party to gather in. Help was sure to be needed with leading the dogs and dragging the bear to the road that was several hard hours away.

I'll never forget how we petted the young pack as we tied them one at a time. The young dogs were improving fast and it was enjoyable conversing with the rest of the party concerning the near future of our inexperienced, but willing-to-learn hounds.

We had a quite difficult time ahead of us, but after several long but enjoyable hours we finally saw chrome on Chick's truck shining in the evening sun and knew for sure that he was glad to see us also. Chick went through his normal routine--petting each dog separately and talking to them as if they were humans. We all loaded up and I remember the kidding about putting me in the front of the truck because of my head cold. Despite their teasing remarks, the cool breeze felt good coming through the windows as we made our way slowly toward the campground.

The club decided over a hot cup of reviving coffee that we had camped long enough and was ready for a night in our regular beds. After breaking camp we were off toward home to show the beautiful coated animal to the women folk, take a few pictures, feed our pack and sit down to a long awaited meal prepared by my mom who could cook with the best of them.

The day had been some kind of hard but the victory was sweet. Deciding to take the next day off from hunting to rest ourselves and the dogs, our club departed. As the last one left, I could think of nothing else but how The Creator had richly blessed a bunch of country boys that day and was truly thankful for enough good health and strength to enjoy a sport such as ours.

As I snickered my way to the house limping on tired, sore legs I suddenly noticed that my head cold was much better. This hunting trip had helped me discover a medicine that needed no prescription.

Glenn Parker at his home in the Little East Fork community.

A TRIP FULL OF SURPRISES

Every time I start thinking back on the 1983 hunting season, I can hardly believe it. My grandpa always promised me that in a lifetime of hunting there would be one particular fall season that stood all alone. There's no doubt that the '83 season breaks all records for memories.

Bear hunting is much like any other sport. Some you win some you loose, and some end tied up. Before detailing the third victorious adventure of the 1983 season, I must come clean and mention one of several hunting trips that ended in defeat.

Our hunting party had hunted two more days of the opening week and hadn't had any luck. We couldn't seem to find bear tracks hot enough for the dogs to smell. As mentioned before, our pack was young and inexperienced especially when it came to staying together while cold trailing for several hours before jumping their prey.

Sunday had rolled around on the colorful October calendar and after a trip to our community churches the hunting party was together again that afternoon. Church was always a part of our weekly concerns and I admire my parents for bringing us boys up in a Baptist believing type of environment. They believed in their heart that God should come first and did everything in their power to see that belief handed down.

When relatively young, most people tend not to appreciate certain establishments in their own community but as time added years on to my life, I began to see things from another point of view. Just recently, the residents of my home community, being led by God, proceeded to renovate the Mount Zion Baptist Church in which I have been a member from childhood.

The renovations took several months to complete and on a weekly basis I was privileged to remember a special moment from my younger days as I observed each portion torn out and rebuilt anew. The Mount Zion Baptist Church building alone will forever be a part of my every being much less the blessings I have received from its members.

The Mount Zion Baptist Church is nestled in a beautiful creek-side setting in the heart of the Dix Creek community. My family resided then, and still does, in the Dix Creek community, which is located in the middle of the Cold Mountain Territory.

Dix Creek is a relatively straight cove that extends from the beautiful river valley of Mundy Field to the high country thickets of the Cold Mountain Swag. Almost all of the real estate included in the Dix Creek area is fine for bear hunting.

Since all of our first week's hunts had been on the West Fork of the Pigeon River, my dad had decided to change territories for the start of the second week of the season. The question could be asked why we hadn't hunted the Dix Creek area during the first week of hunting season since it was closest to our home, but there was a reason.

Along with all of the other teachings of my experienced father, he reminded us that we should never hunt the exact same place two days in a row. He also stated that if bears were plentiful close to home that we should give serious thought to saving those races for later in our season.

By doing that, he explained how two purposes could be served. First, he said this makes other hunters hesitant to even look for bears near our home for they know that we would normally hunt there first. Second, he said, that we should try the far away bears on a round first because every track that our dogs could run was one that a stranger's wouldn't.

The Mount Zion Baptist Church,
a landmark of the Dix Creek Community.

As our team sat together that beautiful Sunday afternoon on the creeping red fescue lawn of home, it was discussed and brought to us young lad's attentions by the veteran hunters that home turf should be the plan for Monday morning which was only hours away. One of the eldest members of our club had talked to a friend who had been hiking in the Dix Creek area. This friend assured him of seeing fresh bear tracks surrounded by plenty of acorns.

Getting off of the subject momentarily, I should explain what acorns and bear hunting could possibly have in common. Believe it or not, black bears' favorite food in the hills of Western North Carolina is acorns. They prefer one certain kind though which is very easily explained. All of the acorns here taste different and I can vouch this accusation truthfully for I have tasted all of them myself. Black Bears' first choice are White Oak and Chestnut Oak acorns. These nuts are fairly mild with a touch of sweetness different from their last choice of Red Oak acorns or Bitter Oak acorns as we home folk call them. Black bears will eat Bitter Oak acorns but they certainly are their last choice.

The deal was discussed and finalized. We would hunt Dix Creek the next morning on Bear Pen Ridge. This ridge, unlike most ridges off of Cold Mountain is very long and straight. It is the divider between Dix Creek and Lenior Creek. To a bear hunter, the most important point on Bear Pen Ridge is located about two thirds of the way up and about equal elevation of the frost line. A small area of Chestnut Oak timber is found there covering approximately three acres of land.

This tract of timber is located in an ideal environment for black bears. The Mountain Ivy there is moderately thick and water is close by also. Black bears like situations such as this because they always go to water after eating and most all of the time lay in Ivy thickets overnight for cover.

Bear Pen Ridge, a keepsake for memories

With the first weeks wire edge off, getting out of bed at 4:30 a.m. would be much harder for the remainder of the season. To get a decent start on a bear hunt, rolling out early is a necessity for there's more to getting ready than most people would realize.

Even though they were young, the dogs became tired after a full week of hunting. Dogs are much like humans. Their pulmonary systems have to gradually become physically fit. By the second week of hunting season, several of them were hard to call out of the warmly bedded doghouses in the early morning hours. Their first few steps on sore, stone-bruised feet seemed to be quite aggravating especially to the few older dogs in the pack.

I'll never forget how patient I was with them during early morning starts. I spoke personally with each and every one and they listened carefully as to understand every word. All of the 1983 pack is gone now to that happy hunting ground and as each one went out in his or her own way, I was sorrowed deep inside. They were like family to me and I will never regret any day that we spent together.

As the dogs were loaded that Monday morning, I distinctly remember my father coming out on his way to work to wish us good luck. As usual, we polished a few last-minute plans with him that could make for a successful hunt and then loaded up to go meet the others.

It was a beautiful morning. The stars could not have been any plainer in that clear October sky. The air was a cool thirty degrees and had a brisk bite about it. That was right down our alley because when the walking begins, a hunter starts heating up quickly even in cold weather.

The old logging road was rocky and rough making vehicle travel slow but we finally parked our pickups at the end of the road on Bear Pen Ridge. After stocking our hunting vests with food and water and replacing the batteries in our small hand-held lights, we started our ascension up the mountain in search of a track that the dogs could smell.

The Bear Pen Trail leaves from the end of the vehicle road and follows the Bear Pen Ridge line all of the way to the High Top Ledge. Several portions of the Bear Pen Ridge Trail make it unforgettable because its periodical steep climbs take most people by surprise.

The Bear Pen Trail intersects on the high top with a path known as The Dix Creek Top Trail. This trail leads to a well known place called The Cold Mountain Swag and from there winds gracefully to the highest peak of Cold Mountain. The elevation on the Cold Mountain Top is six thousand and thirty feet.

During the early morning climb I found myself almost praying for a sudden burst of second wind on the first extremely steep half mile of trail. Not taking any breaks, our hunting party made the initial pull just as scheduled and came into the first gap approximately twenty-five or thirty minutes before daylight.

By that time the steam was rising from the shirt collars of all the hunters and we decided to take a short breather to allow our lungs to catch up with our legs. Our hunting club, as I've stated before, were much like brothers and during the first break along the trail it was a usual thing for somebody to make a joke about another's apparel, such as his boots, his cap, or maybe even the way he was carrying his gun. After several laughs, we began to move again enjoying the flat gap that we were traveling through because the next steep incline was just minutes ahead.

The next climb came soon enough all right as we made our way up the brushy, over-grown trail. The perspiration was streaming from our bodies and my heart was beating in my throat again. Bear Pen Ridge is a tough hunt but we were aware of that fact before we started the journey.

I've never seen a more unique view as what I saw that particular morning after topping out on what is called the Bear Pen Rocks. Off of these rocks visibility is accurate for at least ten miles. The fog was deep in the valley and just as the faintly burning sun was peeping over the eastern horizon, the fog, miles below looked like a lake.

It has always excited me to allow my mind to make believe the shapes of ridge tops, clouds, trees, and such to be that of animals or maybe even people. That morning on the Bear Pen Rocks found my thoughts running wildly as I stared at the imaginary body of water below. I remember how each of us stood there in awe and had surely been blessed if the day had ended at 7:30 a.m.

After a short swallow of water, we proceeded up over the rocks. Just as we were topping the rocky knob into Bear Pen Gap, our dogs stood on their back feet and were suddenly out of control. A bear had undoubtedly crossed the trail just minutes before we had arrived at the rocks.

We backed the dogs hurriedly down the trail away from the strong scent so they would calm down and be less noisy. We were quite confident of the bear's direction but certainly needed to make sure. My brother insisted that we stay put momentarily while he and Sailor checked the track out thoroughly.

Luck wouldn't have had it any better. The dogs had struck the hot track in one of the finest locations on Cold Mountain for hearing a race. I remember how anxious we all were trying to keep the dogs quiet until we heard from my big brother. After about ten nerve racking minutes, I saw his smiling face bursting out of the Laurel coming back to us. Sailor seemed to be most happy too as he excitedly looked toward his teammates. Mark assured us that the bear had gone the usual direction into the right fork of Lenior Creek.

The pack was lined up and ready to go. Adrenaline was flowing freely as we led them up the trail toward the track. Looking ahead I saw my brother unleash Sailor and he took to the brush with lunges of eagerness.

One of the most important segments of bear hunting consists of turning dogs loose properly. When running dogs in a pack, it is an extreme necessity to string them out carefully. Dogs have a natural instinct to try to get ahead of each other when running track scent. Keeping dogs together after unsnapping all of them at the same time is usually a risky proposition. We strung them out perfectly and the race was on.

Some of the hunters started up the trail toward the high top while my brother and I for some unknown reason stayed put to listen for the direction our young pack was to go.

The race sounded so good. They stayed together well and I suddenly got a feeling that the day was going to be very interesting. The dogs trailed flawlessly into the heart of the right fork of Lenior Creek and suddenly jumped their prey.

There's no question when a pack catches up with a bear because they make a totally different sound when looking at a bruin face to face. The heat had definitely been turned up at that point. As the old timer's would say, "This race was hair standing."

After hearing the dogs jump, Mark and I decided to follow directly behind them. The high land of Lenior Creek is very rough and thick. Maneuvering gets to be quite a task after a while of pushing your way through dense Mountain Ivy. The pack left the right fork of Lenior Creek at an unbelievable speed and started their ascent up the congested face of Fork Ridge.

A distant distilled fog lies in a much paralyzed state during the early morning hours in the Western North Carolina valleys making for a unique sight to study.

Fork Ridge separates the right and left forks of Lenior Creek and is as rough as it comes in the mountains of Western North Carolina. The biggest and most vast Laurel and Ivy thickets in the Lenior Creek territory are found on Fork Ridge. When bear hunting this section of Cold Mountain, it's a sure bet for a bear to cross Fork Ridge at least one time in a day.

My brother and I finally made our way to the top of Fork Ridge and heard the pack stopped in the left fork of Lenior Creek. That was comfortable music to our ears for we had temporarily lost hearing of them while climbing the extremely steep mountainside. As we paused briefly, I took a moment to radio Chick on my walkie-talkie who was patiently awaiting our call.

Answering quickly he let us know that the usual way for bear and dogs to run had been and still was silent. When leaving Lenior Creek, bears running from dogs will usually cross a gap call the Stomp. This was the area that Chick had been listening closely to and he was pleased to hear that we had located the pack.

The Stomp Ridge is located on the left side of Lenior Creek and is the divider between it and the Henderson and Anderson Creek sections. From where Chick was located it is possible to hear dogs when crossing the Stomp Ridge which explained why he was so happy to discover from us the location of the pack. We assured him again of their whereabouts and signed off for the action. Chick was so excited that he could hardly talk.

I can't remember ever physically putting out any harder as what my brother and I did for the next fifteen minutes. We were determined to sling a slug and finish polishing the young dogs. Both of us quietly worked the levers on our Winchesters placing live rounds into the chambers when we were about one hundred yards from the action.

Black bears are a long shot from ignorant so slipping carefully to where one is treed is an absolute necessity. We took a few seconds to fully catch our breath and then started in for the kill. I was somewhat concerned about the location of the fellows who had chosen the high top path after the turn loose. It's risky for two people to approach a bear that has been temporarily stopped by hounds, much less four or five.

Bears have a very keen sense of smell therefore human scent is detected by them first and foremost. I figured that our hunting partners were to arrive soon but Mark assured me with a whisper that they hadn't had enough time to make a difference in our strategy.

We slipped very cautiously. For some unknown reason my big brother had put me in front and told me that I was to shoot first. I've known him to do that on several occasions and have always admired his generosity. I gladly accepted the first shot location and felt good in doing so for it had been a year since I had blasted from the pole position.

Getting close enough to see parts of the dogs was so exciting. The opportunity had finally arrived and we suddenly found ourselves about forty feet away from the tree looking with sweat filled eyes expecting to see our black buddy any second. To our surprise the tree was slick and after crawling on our hands and knees close enough to see the dogs plainer, we discovered them looking downward behind a large clump of Mountain Ivy bushes. We knew then that trouble lay ahead.

Getting a shot at a bear on the ground while hunting with dogs is a far from easy task, and is virtually impossible among the thickets of Fork Ridge. At that time, my brother and I decided to separate and close in on the pack from different angles. I crawled the last few feet on my stomach to make little or no noise. Just as black fur became visible to me, the bear leaped into the middle of the pack and made shooting out of the question. We couldn't risk wounding or maybe killing a dog.

In a flash, the young pack left us behind, yelping with every bit of their beings and bounced down the left fork of Lenior Creek. Within a matter of minutes, they were out of our hearing. I can't start to explain what kind of feeling this type of situation puts deep in a bear hunter's chest. We had no choice but to proceed behind them as fast as possible.

From where we were, the closest trail was that of an old logging road that follows Lenior Creek from its mouth all the way to the forks which is a distance of about three miles. The old logging road was close to one-half of a mile below me. The terrain was still as rough and as thick as could be but at least we had downhill for a while. We finally reached the old road very much out of breath and skinned all over.

As my brother and I took a short breather, I turned my hand-held radio on and found poor Chick beside himself. With his excited words running together, he managed to tell us that he could hear the pack fighting hard about two hundred yards on the other side of the creek but still grading downhill.

There was one thing that Chick didn't tell us. Glenn Browning, one of the older hunters in our party had stayed at the truck with him. After hearing the outstanding race, Glenn decided to come down the ridge toward the old logging road hoping to get in on some action.

Until this day, Glenn still enjoys bear hunting as much as any man ever has. He's also a good shot and at that time he could still move through the woods at a pretty good pace. A complete chapter, at least, could be written concerning the physical description and general character of Glenn Browning. He is quite an amazing guy. Glenn is known for his willingness to help people in any situation. He has a very outspoken personality and simply tells it like it is. Glenn is a handy man when it comes to doing chores for the club. Anything asked of him finds Glenn ready and willing and he is an absolute asset to our group.

My brother and I finally made it down the old road enough to regain sound of the dogs. The logging road was virtually free of brush so we could move quickly. As tired as we were getting, our intention was to leave the old road soon enough to grade the mountain at a slight angle which would keep us from having to climb straight uphill to the hounds.

We traveled down the creek further than we realized and found ourselves even with the dogs before we knew it. The mistake had already been made so we wasted no time ascending up a deep little cove toward the roar. Momentarily halting for air, both of us agreed that they were treed this time instead of bayed up.

By then I had almost taken all of the punishment that I could stand and even though he wouldn't admit it, my big brother had too. It was about two hundred yards up the steep brushy incline to where the young pack was hammering. Each step seemed to get a little shorter but we somehow kept on putting new leaves under our feet.

Seeing distance was very much limited again for the Laurel was back in our faces. At approximately fifty feet from the tree the hard trip seemed worth it as both of us spotted the shining black animal high in a Hemlock tree. At that point I'm sure that we were thinking the same thoughts. The Hemlock tree was so limbed that shooting was to be difficult.

Glenn Browning, a unique individual

I remember my brother and I looking at each other with overheated confused faces. Suddenly, a thirty-caliber blast echoed the cove bringing us to our knees. The bear instantly rolled down through the popping and cracking Hemlock limbs and softly met the ground among the deserving young pack.

Not knowing who had done the shooting, Mark and I hurried under the tree and looked Glenn straight in the face. We were so happy that it was him and by his expression we knew that the feeling was mutual.

The bear had a beautiful coat. While admiring it and checking the dogs carefully for injuries, we heard a strange noise in the Hemlock above us. We looked up quickly and to our surprise found that one of the dogs had climbed the tree trying to get to the bear. He seemed awfully confused and couldn't figure his way down for the victory celebration. After laughing until we hurt, my brother climbed the tree and rescued him. Following a good long rest we started making our way back toward the old roadbed.

I'll never forget how touched I was when we radioed to Chick. He had heard it all from where he stood and was so emotional that he could hardly speak. I can imagine how he must have felt after listening to the roar for at least an hour and not being physically able to do anything about it. That really hurt me but I knew he was proud of us and at the time that's all that mattered. Before signing off, Chick assured us that he would take his pickup to the mouth of Lenior Creek and wait patiently to give the tired party a ride.

A short time later the rest of the hunters gathered in to help with leading the pack and dragging the bear. We had good fellowship together and that's what really counts, especially in the modernized times in which we live today.

The adventure had been a tough one and was still a ways from being over. While resting for a short spell and eating what few snacks we had left, we all regained a portion of our strength and started making our way down the rugged old road.

Late in the afternoon hours, our tired party of hunters finally made it to Chick's truck. As usual, he was overly glad to see us and congratulated each of us on a fine day in the woods. My mind will always keep the memory of how happy Chick would get every time a bear was harvested. He would pet the hounds softly while looking at each one closely for cuts or bruises. Chick had a special way of communicating with the young pack and they seemed to understand his caring disposition.

After getting out of the woods, there's still a lot of work to be done when a bear has been taken. The carcass has to be skinned and cleaned properly and butchered for freezing. The dogs are overly anxious for food and antibiotics have to be administered to the ones who were misfortunate in receiving bites. Our hunting party has always worked together in achieving those chores and enjoyed reliving the day's hunt again and again.

After finishing our last minute responsibilities of the farm, my brother and I laid down on the cement driveway flat on our backs and looked toward the sky quietly. Nothing else could have been said about our outdoor adventure that day. My big brother looked tiredly at me and softly said, "What a trip." We helped each other up and slowly made our way toward an irresistible aroma that was coming from the kitchen belonging to the best cook ever.

My mom, Barbara Griffin, shown here in her kitchen.
She has prepared many good meals there and has always met her
family's needs.

BOUND AND DETERMINED

The kitchen seemed to be silent. The only sound the house could acquire was that of water boiling peacefully on the stove. Steam flowed gracefully from the battered old kettle as my brother and I sat at the eating table lacing our boots.

Mom was the first to speak gingerly asking what we had in mind for breakfast at such an early hour. I'll forever admire my mother for how she always saw us off properly whether it be to work or to play. She never let us leave without seeing that our eating and clothing needs were met.

After a delicious home-cooked breakfast consisting of country-cured bacon and farm-fresh eggs, Mark and I made our way through the brisk morning air toward the dog lot where sounds of eagerness filled the air. The pack seemed to be overly ready for hunting that particular morning and was prompt to load themselves when unsnapped from their chains.

Without a distinct plan, we drove to our regular morning meeting place to find a skeleton crew of hunters gathered purchasing drinks and snacks for the day's hunt. Our small community store was owned and operated at that time by Mr. and Mrs. Frank Blaylock. They never opened up for business later than 5:30 a.m. I guess that's the main reason we met there for we could buy last minute items and sometimes plan our hunts both at the same time. Mr. and Mrs. Blaylock worked hard all of their lives but always seemed to take time to talk to people, whether it be a neighbor or a stranger.

As we began to discuss our plans that morning it was evident that none of us had any promising ideas. We all looked to Chick that morning for much needed advice. I remember him saying that he would like to hear another race on Lenior Creek. Chick liked to hunt that area because he could get his truck high enough in that place to hear parts of the race if a track to run could be found. So it was settled. We were off to Bear Pen Ridge again.

As said earlier, the dogs seemed to be very eager to hunt that morning because they had rested for a total of three days. The last hunt had been a hard one for both men and dogs so taking time to rest was a necessity. When bear packs are not in shape to hunt with full potential, not going at all is usually the best bet. For that reason we had taken two days off from hunting to give the dogs adequate time to revive.

When the crack of dawn came the trucks were parked and our hunting party was working aggressively up the first big incline. As I've mentioned earlier, Bear Pen Trail is one of the steepest grades in the Cold Mountain Territory and is a muscle buster first thing in the morning.

The best I recollect, there were only five of us hunting that morning. When bear hunting with that few people, the circumstance calls for each man to lead four dogs instead of the usual two. That made the steep incline a touch easier. Because of their eagerness to run, the dogs helped by pulling on the leashes. It's sometimes surprising how just a few extra pounds of pulling power can make a body feel lighter on steeply- graded mountain trails.

As the usual sweat began to bead and my lungs caught second wind, I felt as though I could have run ten miles without stopping. I was ready for a race. All we needed was a hot fresh track.

Mr. and Mrs. Frank Blaylock, friendly people who have helped
our community for many years. The country store that they
owned and operated seven days per week was handy to say the
least.

Along the trail the party had to break momentarily on the rocks of Bear Pen for our morning look at the awesome creation of the beautiful Mundy Field Valley far below. I've said it before and will proudly say it again, that each time I look off from these rocks at the view below, I realize the power of the Creator above. The view is breath taking especially just after dawn on a clear October morning.

Luck wouldn't have it for us that particular morning as it did on the last hunt, for we left the rocks and ascended the ridge onto Bear Pen Knob without finding even a faint smell of a bear. Dropping into the deep Bear Pen Gap, we decided to grade downward in a southern direction toward the water of the Right Prong of Lenior Creek.

With Sailor and Timber, a young pup, out in front my brother and I proceeded a small distance ahead of the pack through the ideal oak feeding grounds. Timber seemed to be our pick for taking the responsibilities of a strike dog. Sailor was ten years old at the time and not wanting to think about it, we all knew that this season would surely finish his career.

Training a young pup to strike bears while on a leash is a difficult proposition. There's more to it than most folk could comprehend. It takes a lot of patience and many blown out hunting days to train a strike dog to be successful. We all had faith that Timber could do it for he surely had all of the capabilities to perform well at finding tracks and keeping his mouth shut while working them.

Through the large Chestnut Oak timber, bear tracks were plentiful but none of them seemed to be smellable to the dogs. Some of the tracks looked to Mark and I to have been made within the last twelve hours and while taking a small break we started discussing why the dogs wouldn't pay any attention to them.

The Mountain Laurel and Ivy bushes were as wet that clear morning as if it had rained overnight. The fog had settled in the big cove in which we were hunting and seemed to be the primary reason for the bear tracks being scentless. The woods were suddenly dripping wet and other plans were to be made if we were to get a bear up and running.

The Fork Ridge that lays in the head of Lenior Creek consists of dense Mountain Laurel thickets in which most bears residing in the area stay at night after feeding hours. Knowing this, we hurriedly made plans to cross the Right Prong Creek and proceed into them. Leading dogs on Fork Ridge is very difficult, but is possible if you can manage to keep your cool when finding yourself wrapped up in Laurel limbs and your dog leash hung around several bushes all at the same time. The terrible journey through the rough would be worth it though if we could find a hot track.

The rugged, overgrown thicket had taken its toll on time that particular morning for moving through the smothery limbs had taken longer than planned. With our clothes wet and our patience to a bare minimum, our party had to stop temporarily for another breather. Little did we know that luck was about to turn our way.

After a few sips of water and a nibble of candy, we proceeded on toward the top of Fork Ridge. Just before topping out the pack suddenly exploded with barks and leaps as to get loose any way they could. There was nothing we could do at that point but unsnap all of them for we surely had made our way straight to a bear bed.

It's hard to explain the feeling of excitement when the dogs are unleashed unexpectedly. As they quickly faded up Fork Ridge, we all started figuring out the best path to the Cold Mountain Swag for that was definitely our only way to find out which way the pack was destined. From where we had turned loose, the shortest way to The Swag was up Fork Ridge. That was to be an adventure of its own for the thickets of Fork Ridge are unchanging from bottom to top.

Before we turned the pack loose my brother told me of how he seemed to be feeling ill. At this point he was sure of it. He promised to be all right and another hunter agreed to stay along with him so I left them and started climbing Fork Ridge alone. I vowed to him that I would do my best to locate the dogs and radio as soon as possible.

I was still feeling like a million bucks and was ready for the long ascension of the thick ledge. About halfway up, my legs and back began to tire but I kept reaching down deep inside myself for another blast of energy. I was bound and determined to reach The Swag of Cold Mountain. The steady pull lasted and lasted. After several short stops for breath, and about fifty minutes later, I could see the sky light through the tall Laurel toward the high top. Seeing imprints of ridge tops through the dense timber always makes me feel better for when that happens, relief from climbing is getting much closer.

Bursting out into the brown, frost bitten fields of The Cold Mountain Swag, and after my heart quieted in my ears, I began to listen for the pack. To my surprise, they were closer than I ever would have dreamed and were solid treed every breath. It was too good to be true.

I distinctly remember the talk that I had with myself in which no thoughts could be found for ever treeing a bear where our dogs were presently treed. In fact, I had never been exactly where they were but memories of my dad's stories let me know that it was rough real estate.

The mixed pine and hardwood ridge line of Rip Shin pictured here ranks above the best for memories when the Crawford's Creek side of Cold Mountain is mentioned.

The dogs were treed high on the Crawford's Creek side of Cold Mountain on a well-known ridge called Rip Shin. Rip Shin Ridge has characteristics much like the high country ridges in the Western parts of the United States. It's covered with low growing trees and Mountain Ivy and from the overlooking rocks on the top of Cold Mountain, looks quite awesome. The blend of the natural yellow, red, and green colors of an October morning was splendid.

There is a well-known trail that passes through The Cold Mountain Swag called the path to Shining Rock. The Shining Rock Trail is traveled quite often by hunters and hikers and follows the leading ridge between The East Fork and West Fork sections of The Pigeon River.

There are several specific points on this trail that have been named by hunters and old timers of the past which are still called the same. Leaving the Cold Mountain Swag toward Shining Rock, the first named point is the Cold Mountain Spring. Many people have enjoyed the pure mountain water that runs freely out of the granite rock at that location.

The pack was treed above the Cold Mountain Spring and just on the Crawford's Creek side of Cold Mountain. Instead of traveling down the trail to the spring, I decided to grade evenly around the rocky ridge toward the steady roar.

The elevation where the dogs were stopped is approximately fifty-eight hundred feet. Knowing this made me aware of the fact that the timber there wasn't big at all. That was a disadvantage to me because as a usual thing, bears will tree in big timber especially if they have taken a tree to stay. Knowing that the trees were relatively small in the area, the bear would most likely try its best to exit the scene at the first smell of a human.

Slipping at my absolute best ability, I crawled within one hundred feet of the hammering pack. Just as I saw black in the small Red Oak tree, it suddenly disappeared as I had figured would happen. Disheartened and physically exhausted, all that I could do was listen to them descend into The Crawford's Creek Valley below.

I was hoping with all of my being that the pack would start turning one way or the other because staying straight bound for the water on Crawford's Creek would make for an almost sure getaway. They didn't turn either way and after crossing the creek, went as a bear usually does after making its final decision to exit the Cold Mountain section for good.

The small cove that the dogs had speeded down is known as Turkey Pen. As I have written in the previous paragraph, the day would have been much easier if the dogs could have turned one way or the other. If they had gone to the left, they would have crossed the Rip Shin Ridge that was mentioned earlier, into the Pine Stand, Elb Gap, and Basin Branch areas of Cold Mountain. When a bear chooses that route to run, they are definitely going to a rougher, more suitable fighting terrain but in turn makes it much easier on the hunter.

The Cold Mountain top is high above all of the other ridges and coves and is sharply pointed so to speak. When topping out as far as humanly possible, staying in hearing of the dogs is easy. All a hunter has to do is pace back and forth no more than one hundred and fifty feet and listen to bear hound packs as they cover miles of country in very short lengths of time.

Bears running from dogs in this direction are destined for a particular cove that is densely covered in Ivy and lays on the north slopes of Cold Mountain called Cold Creek. When crossing out of the Pine Stand, Elb Gap, and Basin Branch areas of Crawford's Creek, dogs go into the Cold Creek area because it is bear's favorite territory for fighting and for using the rough terrain to their advantage.

They'll usually cross the high top of Cold Mountain through a small gap called Basin Gap or a place just above Basin Gap known as Green Knob. Cold Creek is where most bear races end if victory is scheduled in a hunter's good luck quest for the day.

Cold Creek is without a doubt the most rugged and Ivy-covered tributary of Cold Mountain. It's well known in these parts for its rocky, rough conditions. Many bear races have ended in defeat in the Cold Creek area, for it takes a devoted pack to make it from one side to the other especially when passing after twelve noon. Cold Creek is where tired dogs with fast dwindling energy will fall out of bear races. On the other hand, if a pack has enough energy left to hustle when crossing into Cold Creek, bears will sometimes climb and climb to stay.

If our pack had taken a right turn out of Turkey Pen Cove, they would have been out of hearing quickly but could have been found just as easy.

On the Shining Rock Trail that leaves from the Cold Mountain Swag toward Shining Rock, the second-named point after passing the Cold Mountain Spring is called the Dock Patch. The Dock Patch is nothing special to see but dogs leaving out of Turkey Pen Cove to the right side looking down will without a doubt cross through The Dock Patch. When doing so, they enter a vast cove of the Little East Fork section called Sorrell's Creek. From there they can go several different directions. They can go deeper into the Little East Fork section toward Fork Mountain or stay to the right continuously and cross into the Schoolhouse Branch and Murray Cove areas.

Understanding the geographical lay of the Cold Mountain tributaries may seem difficult to comprehend, but is made easier as stated previously by Cold Mountain's cone shaped top of which a few hundred yards heads up miles and miles of ridges and coves between the two forks of the Pigeon River.

Cold Creek's rugged and Ivy covered ridges are unforgettable for those who have ventured among them.

Unfortunately our pack didn't turn left or right. They stayed straight ahead and entered one of the most difficult places in Western North Carolina to stay up with dogs or even to track dogs with modernized tracking collars, which we didn't have at that time. They went down Turkey Pen Cove and crossed through a very well-known place in the Crawford's Creek section called Frady's Orchard.

Frady's Orchard is a private piece of property relatively high up on Crawford's Creek and joins the Shining Rock Wilderness, and is not publicly accessible by vehicle. Facing up Crawford's Creek this piece of property is located at the mouth of the last cove on the left called Birch Spring Hollow.

The next cove to the left of Birch Spring Hollow is known as John's Cove. John's Cove covers many acres of land and is the last cove in The Crawford's Creek area before crossing into the Big East Fork section of the Pigeon River. The dividing ridge between John's Cove and Birch Spring Hollow is known as Dog Loser and the information that I have already penned, makes it understandable as to why the name fits perfectly.

When my heart finally went from my throat back to my chest, I struck a grade around the rocky mountainside figuring to enter The Shining Rock Trail about the Dock Patch. I didn't stand a chance keeping up with the pack by following behind them so the Shining Rock Trail was the only choice I had. Almost in sight of it, I stopped to listen and the dogs begin to sound a bit louder as they gradually ascended Dog Loser Ridge. Even though they were far away I could still hear their echoing voices plain for the higher they went the better the quality of sound became.

I've heard bear packs climb Dog Loser Ridge many times in my life and knew what would happen when the pack finally topped out. When dogs cross the big round topped ridge into the John's Cove area of Crawford's Creek, their sound can disappear instantly and from that point guesswork comes into play for the rest of the hunting day.

I didn't want to leave the Dock Patch until I had made a decent guess of which angle they were to go out of my hearing. To my surprise the pack suddenly stopped just across Dog Loser Ridge on the John's Cove side and to my grateful ears started hammering out tree barks again. I was astounded to hear them treed again but also sorrowful inside by knowing that there was little to no hope for me to get there before dark.

At that point, I was too far down the Shining Rock Trail for my hand-held radio to successfully transmit to the other hunters who were still climbing Fork Ridge on Lenior Creek. I was beside myself as I jumped from rock to rock down the steep trail from the Dock Patch to the next named point of the Shining Rock Trail called the Deep Gap.

Dog Loser Ridge seen here in the distance lies quietly in the upper most portion of the Crawford's Creek area.

Still with no radio reception, I hot footed through the Deep Gap with a small glimmer of hope to some way get to the pack that was several hard hours away. The best way to the dogs from where I was located was to follow the trail to Shining Rock itself and from there follow The Old Butt Trail out The Big East Fork ledge which would pass me by the head of Dog Loser Ridge. The only problem with that plan was several hard miles laid ahead of my already stiff and tired legs.

Stopping at the next named point on the Shining Rock Trail called the Narrows found me trying to think of a better solution to a fast arising problem. The Narrows on the Shining Rock Trail is a unique place to see. It's literally named correct for the mountain ledge there is sharply pointed. The ridge is narrowed down to three or four feet wide for a distance of approximately one hundred yards. Its character is made whole by the large boulders sticking out of the ground making passage somewhat confined. Leaned against one of the huge rocks, I decided to try my hand-held again.

The first transmission I made, a voice of excitement blundered out of the small radio speaker and Chick's acknowledgment made my day. As he always did, Chick had figured that I had been gone too long and knew where to go. He had located himself at a well-known point in the Crawford's Creek section of Cold Mountain called the Maple Ford.

At that particular time, the Maple Ford was as far as a vehicle was allowed up Crawford's Creek. His first request was to know if I had a location on the pack and I was sure enough glad to tell him the story. I asked him if by any chance did he have someone with him that was able to walk a good distance up John's Cove Creek to the tired pack.

The Deep Gap and the Narrows Ridge seen in the distance here
ages to a more beautiful sight year after year.

Luck couldn't have had it be better because Chick
had picked his eldest son up on the way and had him by his
side. The thought had occurred to me earlier of how I would
like to have a fresh man over in the John's Cove area to
answer me on my hand-held CB. Hearing from Chick and
knowing that he had a healthy, hardy man with him was
surely a God send.

I quickly told him to send his son up by the Old
Reece house that sits in the immediate forks of Crawford's

Creek and John's Cove Creek, and follow the John's Cove Creek until he came into hearing of the dogs. He promised that he would and there was nothing else I could do but wait and listen to the slowed-down barks of a fine young pack of canines.

The other hunters had topped out by that time and made their way hurriedly down the trail toward the Deep Gap. By radio, I told them where I was and they came on to The Narrows for a better listen to the exhausted dogs.

I guess the wait seemed longer than it really was but by that time, the usual anxiety had gotten the best of my tired body. From the rocks of the Narrows we listened quietly waiting for the Winchester echo to blast our way. I've written previously of how waiting on another hunter to make the counting move is most emotional. Tense wasn't a good word to describe us that late afternoon, for Chick's son was our only hope.

The pack seemed to pick up their barking pace after a long, nervous hour. We knew that he was close then and was on edge for sure. Finally, the blast of relief echoed across Dog Loser Ridge and all of us sighed at once. Chick's son had a hand-held and although his transmission was scratchy, we understood enough to know that he had finished the job.

We all started back to the Deep Gap and lined down the trail of Crawford's Creek to the mouth of John's Cove. At that point, we weren't far from Chick's pickup truck but we turned up the John's Cove Trail with a new glimmer of strength to meet Henry's son and aid him in any way possible for he had surely been the man of the day.

The long pull of John's Cove Creek was longer than normal because of our fatigue. It was dusky dark when the first sight of a hound was discovered. Having no choice,

Chick's son had left the dogs loose after the kill. He had a big enough challenge ahead of him as it was to get the bear carcass down the steep ridge into an old logging road that was built parallel to John's Cove Creek in the mid-1900's. We had hoped that he could at least get it to the creek and we were thankful when he came into sight. He was glad to see us too and needless to say we congratulated him on a job well done.

The batteries in our small hand-held lights were weak from morning's use but beat nothing by a long shot. After putting the dogs on leashes and petting them thoroughly, we took turns for several hard hours pulling the bear carcass. Finally, we made it to the Maple Ford to find Chick absolutely filled to the rim with joy. As usual, Chick's emotions were second to none on a happy scale.

As we rode the pickup down the rocky road of Crawford's Creek, we couldn't have been happier and I remember us giving credit to our fast improving young pack of dogs.

Sailor had laid down in the bed of the truck immed-iately after loading and had his tired head on his front paws. Nothing about him moved but his big brown eyes. His hunting days were almost over and I know he was aware of that fact, but as he looked at me, I also knew that he was proud. I pulled Sailor into my lap and stroked him grace-fully.

My happiness had been temporarily postponed by Sailor's tired disposition and as we continued to ride, I knew that he was aware of how much I thought of him even though the young pack wasn't depending on him as they once did. He had done his job well. As he drifted off to sleep on my lap, I felt something roll down my cheek and my bottom lip began to quiver.

Holding the old dog close all the way home, good memories of him ran wildly through my mind. He was surely a legend in his time and knowing that he was quickly approaching retirement, his character still conveyed a most positive message of being bound and determined.

NEVER GIVE UP

The sunshine seemed warmer than normal for the later part of October as we found shade beneath the Red Maple tree that grows directly in front of the home place. This particular day had been consumed by the chore of lawn mowing. In years past, the lawn wasn't very big but Dad had cleared more and more land until grass cutting had become an all-day project.

Along with the teachings of hunting to the best of our abilities, my father tried with all his heart to teach us boys to work diligently at whatever we did and to strive for improvement on a steady basis. Through the years I have seen his beliefs proved right many times and can think back of how my grandpa's farm was quite run down when my dad and mother settled us in Smokey Cove to call it home.

Smokey Cove is a relatively small tributary of Dix Creek and has been good to a country boy such as myself, from my boyhood to raising a kid of my own. The present finds the rolling pasture hills of Smokey Cove green and free from briers, thistles and wild roses but they weren't always that way. After moving us into a new log home in Smokey Cove, my mother and father had a lot of challenges facing them to get the old home place neat and free from unwanted debris. Being younger boys at the ages of fifteen and twelve, my brother and I didn't understand this weedy row that our mother and father had chosen to hoe.

The two-story farmhouse that my grandparents, Elbert and Sally Griffin, had resided in for over thirty-five years was still structurally sound but needed renovating inside and out. The big barn was also sound but needed everything from exterior lumber to new paint on the roof.

The pastureland consisted of forty to fifty acres and needed lots of work. The wire fences were old and the yellow locust stakes were rotten from years of service. Water was a problem in several places on the farm and many ditches were to be dug and hundreds of feet of pipe were to be laid to drain those places properly.

The home place of Mr. and Mrs. Elbert Griffin

The old two-story house is still precious to me as I remember many fine occasions spent with my grandparents there.

Seen here is the big barn that belongs with the home place of my grandparents. It is still in use and is structurally sound. Its presence has seen many crops come and go along with some of the best farm animals that ever was trained to wear a harness.

My father worked a public job at a large paper mill in the small town of Canton, North Carolina. I now look back and wonder how he found the time and energy to keep on progressing at the much needed maintenance of the small farm. I can remember him working the graveyard shift and after sleeping as little as two hours, be out and about working diligently at whatever job he had chosen to do.

My brother and I couldn't understand why all of this work had to be done constantly year in and year out with the exception of six to seven weeks of bear hunting. After maturing a bit, I distinctly remember the day that I started to comprehend my dad's thoughts.

One morning we were on the south side of the farm grubbing briers and piling them with hay forks. My young mood was down that morning and was fairly depressed with nothing to look forward to but cutting and piling briers for the remainder of the day.

Being the one in the family to speak out, I finally got enough nerve to ask my dad why we were trying to clear the land at such a fast pace and also proceeded to verbally estimate at least a five-year work plan to finish if we were lucky. I knew that I had said too much the second that the last word came out of my mouth.

If I live to be ninety-five years old, I'll never forget what my father said to me that brisk morning as he wiped the sweat from his forehead. "Son," he said, "always remember what I'm going to say. Whatever you set out to do, make sure that you do it right and work with a chest full of faith to see you through the finish. Never give up at anything. God saw fit for us to have this place so the least we can do is decorate for him." From that day forward, I started to understand my dad's thoughts and felt much better about helping with the duties of our small farm nestled in the heart of Smokey Cove.

We had decided that a couple of day's rest was necessary for the dogs because the last hunt had been extremely hard on them. Time wasn't really a factor to me anyway for the farming season was over and the fall season brought with it the chore of firewood cutting, which I enjoyed greatly.

The log house in which we lived was and still is heated with a wood furnace located in its underground basement. In my opinion, no other heat can compare with wood. It's exceptionally clean also if the airflow is filtered and ducted properly.

My father and I enjoy cutting firewood together and don't consider it to be work, but a pleasure. It's very good exercise and a nice Locust wood fire on a chilly October night makes for a cozy environment when sipping on fresh hot coffee while watching World Series Baseball games on television.

The hunters gathered at our place late in the afternoon on Wednesday of bear season's second week to discuss plans for a Thursday hunt. We all agreed that the Cold Mountain area had been hunted enough for a few days and plans for our next hunting escapade should be made for another location.

Acorns were plentiful in the West Fork section of the Pigeon River and the members of the hunting party leaned heavily toward there for the next hunt. In a previous chapter, I have written information about the West Fork section of the Pigeon River and have mentioned the Fork Mountain area briefly. It is a vast mountainous region of Sherwood Forest and is free from vehicle travel.

Seen here is the log house in which I was privileged to help build as a young boy. Many hard hours were spent erecting it, which is important to my memories today. I admire my parents for taking on such a project and it remains something to be proud of for my family.

Fork Mountain separates The Little East Fork and the West Fork of the Pigeon River. Fork Mountain is approximately seven miles long. It extends from the Shining Rock Wilderness road in the high elevated grasslands to the Lake Logan Dam, located where the river forks join together on highway 215 about ten miles south of the small town of Canton.

The Fork Mountain Trail follows the huge ridge top over halfway down it and is of good quality. It leaves the top of Fork Mountain in a gap called Turnpike and winds back and forth down the steep mountainside into the river at The Sunburst Campground, which is approximately two miles south of Lake Logan.

The old trail continues from Turnpike Gap out the leading ridge of Fork Mountain to a site that used to be well known in that area. The Fork Mountain Fire Tower was located there years ago. It has since been dismantled and the old trail is very difficult to find, much less stay in for any length of time.

Turnpike was where we decided to try on Thursday morning and felt sure of finding a hot track to run. That Thursday hunt was unlucky all the way around for nothing went right. I'm sure that it was mostly human error though, because the track we had put the dogs on was too old to run.

The pack cold trailed out of Turnpike into the next cove up called Big Rock House. Out of Big Rock House Cove, they proceeded into the next parallel cove up the Pigeon River called Little Rock House. They turned up the steep cove and crossed the Fork Mountain Trail into the Little East Fork area.

As mentioned before, the Little East Fork of the Pigeon River is big country. Its most narrow point is known as Camp Daniel Boone but strangely opens up wider and wider for at least two miles upstream before coming to a close in the Cherry Cove area of the Shining Rock Wilderness. From the Cherry Cove area, we lost hearing of the dogs. While in his vehicle on the Blue Ridge Parkway, Chick positioned himself to vaguely hear a few barks but quickly lost them into a vast area known as Davidson River.

No more can be said about that lost day. It was for sure, when bear hunting in those parts, or any other parts for that reason we couldn't win every time we went hunting. That day ended a loss and dark found us still looking for three of the dogs. In the night hours we finally found the last one and headed for home. Naturally, we rested our pack on Friday but big plans were already made for a Saturday hunt. My dad and I noticed lots of bear tracks while trying to stay up with the fast moving dogs on Thursday.

At that time, our Hunting Club included several young boys that strictly loved to bear hunt but weekdays were off limits for them because of school. They all looked forward to Saturdays during bear season for they were free for the most part and open for business when bear hunting was mentioned. Our weekday skeleton crew of hunters enjoyed Saturdays also. That meant extra dog leaders were on tap, which made bear hunting trips much easier.

Viewed in this photo is Looking Glass Rock, a popular portion of the Davidson River area of Transylvania County in Western North Carolina.

To my surprise, after talking to the young boys on Friday night, one of them was all that could hunt on Saturday. The others were disappointed but their families had other plans that included them for the weekend. Some of the older hunters were to be absent on Saturday also and an unusually small crew showed the next morning to hunt.

A cold front had slipped into the Western North Carolina region overnight and gave Saturday morning's thermometers their lowest readings of the season. The air had a bite as we loaded the dogs that morning. The colder it is, the more eager they are to go.

I've laughed many times on cold mornings as I watched the hounds pay me little to no attention because of their anxiety. Those actions usually calls for discipline to finally be administered.

I've never been one to handle dogs in an abusive kind of way but corrective action must be taken with hunting dogs if they are to be successful. Dogs are smart animals although they are much like humans in letting bad habits become a part of their day-to-day living.

After stocking our hunting vests with supplies at Frank's Country Store, we were off. If we would have known what kind of day lay in store for us that morning, I'm sure some members of the party would have looked forward to it and some would have dreaded it. My dad had a plan for our Saturday morning adventure and little did I know just how tough it was going to be. The ridge he had chosen to take the pack up had never been foot printed by me before.

Up Highway 215, about halfway between Lake Logan and the Blue Ridge Parkway lies a ridge to the left of the Pigeon River called Bird Stand.

Bird Stand is different from all of the other ridges on the left side of the Pigeon because of its vast cliffs. I'm sure these cliffs are of granite but through time have faded to a dark bluish shade. Their color seems to be a touch lighter in winter than in summer and they are uniquely shaped.

Bird Stand Ridge, seen here holds characteristics that stand alone compared to the rest of the ridges on the West Fork of the Pigeon River. Its vast rock cliffs are somewhat misleading when looking upon them from Highway 215 far below.

As I recall, there were only four of us on the drive that morning and Chick was on the road below in his pickup. The first trial was crossing the river while leading dogs with both hands and trying to keep our balance on the slick rocks. The river was running bigger than normal that morning due to a hard Friday shower and the rocks were covered with a skim of overnight ice.

After looking the slippery situation over cautiously, we proceeded to throw sand on the icy rocks so our boots could gain more traction. We all crossed the river safely and started the steep climb not knowing exactly what the next two hours held for us.

Close to the river, the Laurel and Ivy wasn't unbearably thick but the further we went the worse it seemed to get. We didn't take any breaks for at least one hard hour until we suddenly came out of the thicket onto one of the cliff-like parts of the ridge. Our small party stopped momentarily at the long awaited opening for much needed body cooling.

Perspiration had begun to work its way through our clothing and I distinctly remember how we snickered at each other as we steamed in the cool morning air. We could see Highway 215 from our stopping point on Bird Stand Ridge and figured ourselves to be about halfway up the rocky, steep ledge.

The dogs hadn't shown even a remote clue of smelling a bear and the steep Mountain Ivy thicket had taken a toll on our energy levels in a hurry. As we sat on the solid rock ledge overlooking the Wash Hollow and Fire Scald area of the West Fork, I couldn't help but feel slightly depressed about our Saturday hunt.

I started complaining to my dad for choosing such a rough route for our hunt that day and even made a frowning gesture or two insinuating that we might have been in the wrong place for a successful Saturday bear race seeing that tracks had been scarce so far.

As he always would, my father explained to me that cool, brisk, morning of how hunting with dogs challenged a person from within and assured me that our Saturday adventure in the woods was a long shot from being over. He knew how to make tired bodies feel better instantly. I've known him to do that many times.

Through all of the years that I've been with him in the woods, I've never seen him get down and out. He seems to keep an optimistic opinion all of the time. As we got back to our feet and untied the pack from the small saplings above the cliff, I'll never forget what my dad's last sentence consisted of before breaking brush again. "Boys, don't ever give up until you put the dogs back in the truck."

With no trail, Bird Stand Ridge lasted and lasted that Saturday morning but constantly thinking back of my dad's optimistic words of hope made me chuckle between mad spells of being tangled and hung up by dense Laurel and Ivy limbs. No breaks were in sight from the vast thicket but we kept on striving for the elevated Fork Mountain Trail.

At last, we could see the high top we had endured for and with sweat-soaked clothing, stopped just before twelve noon on a black strip of rocks for lunch. The view from there was absolutely breath taking as we observed how gracefully the West Fork of the Pigeon wound up the valley below. Highway 215 looked to be as small as an ant trail from where we sat.

Our bodies finally cooled and after our hunger pains were taken care of, we proceeded on to the top of Fork Mountain and into its wide-open trail. All of us talked for at least fifteen minutes concerning how nice it was to walk in a path again after being out of one since dawn.

On the Fork Mountain Trail, we made our way in an easterly direction through Little Rock House Gap and then on to Big Rock House Gap. We were exhausted but while being stopped to rest, I noticed my dad to be feeling much better than me and heard him repeat not to lose hope for bear striking was still a good possibility.

I wish to halt the momentum of this story moment-arily to mention how grateful I am to still be physically able to take my dogs hunting in the Fork Mountain area of Sherwood Forest. Being fifteen years later, I am penning these words on a day that has seen me fortunate enough to be on the Fork Mountain Trail again. I stood in awe just before noon today and recollected my memories of this chapter from high above the West Fork of the Pigeon River on Bird Stand Ridge. As I was observing the area closely, I caught myself daydreaming of my young condition on that cool morning in 1983 and personally thanked God for the strength to return again with no abnormal health difficulties other than moving at a slower pace.

To our surprise, about two hundred yards from where we had rested, Sailor jerked my dad out of the trail. We turned the pack immediately and took them back up the trail a good distance as to quieten them down. Dad was ecstatic and hurriedly snapped Sailor to my lead in place of the young pup Timber. He quickly explained how using Timber to discover the direction of the track would be good training for him. Returning in a few minutes, he claimed to be ready for the pack and we proceeded back down the trail toward the piping hot scent.

Luck had offered me a very strange equation that particular day and finding the correct formula to successfully work it was to be most trying. When bear hunting with dogs in Western North Carolina, a hunter stands a much greater chance for quality production from his pack if they can be put on a track early in the day. In my past years of bear hunting, I've seen very little positive results from turning bear packs loose after 12:00 noon. This was on my mind heavily as we strolled down the Fork Mountain Trail to finally unsnap our hounds.

I quickly noticed Sailor's actions as we approached the point where the bear had crossed the trail. He winded with his nose constantly toward the Little East Fork side of Fork Mountain and not knowing what Dad had earlier discovered made me pay him no attention. After reaching our turn loose destination, I strangely noticed the young trainee pulling my dad vigorously toward the West Fork side of the Fork Mountain ledge. His actions were directly opposite of the projected path that Sailor had already decided upon.

I immediately foresaw problems arising for us at great speed, especially when I mentioned Sailor's actions to Dad just seconds before we were to unsnap the hounds. He quickly brought to my attention the fact of Sailor's age and that he had probably made the wrong decision concerning the direction in which the bear had crossed the trail. My father was confident of Timber's conclusion so we proceeded to unyoke the pack in single file into the Turnpike area of the West Fork. Sailor wasn't overly enthused about the situation but made his way slowly toward the excited barks of his already distant teammates.

To my surprise, the pack sounded good as they always do a few minutes after unleashing them. They seemed to be staying together well but as more and more time went by we started to realize that something was wrong.

When bear packs run in the wrong direction, their smelling abilities have no choice but to finally be dissipated. The further they go, the less the quality of the scent becomes making the track colder and colder as they put more and more land under their feet. Bear hunters call this situation back tracking and it makes for a sure hunting-day failure unless dogs can be recovered relatively quick and made to run the other way.

After a hard hour's work, we finally caught the dogs. Admitting to our mistakes we quickly proceeded to put their noses on the right end of the track. Sailor was correct even in his old age and the hounds went onto the Little East Fork side of Fork Mountain tracking perfectly. I remember my dad and I watching them as they barked evenly through the open woods before entering a dense thicket that had already been darkened by the afternoon shade.

It was hard for me to believe what all had come to pass that Saturday from the first light of day until the present. I chuckled to myself as the dogs faded lower and lower down the Little East Fork side of Fork Mountain just thinking of what might happen next.

Our hunting trips were usually very well organized and quite formal but this one had been much of a wreck so far. We had experienced an awful day in the woods but the fine race that we were hearing had a way of making us forget our misfortunes in a hurry.

Any number of outcomes could have occurred in the next few seconds. Anxiety levels were at a usual high as we listened to the pack trail on. My dad and I enjoyed the proud feeling we acquired as we waited quietly for the dogs to explode so to speak when the bear was jumped out of the laying ground. Several minutes went by and all of us stood silently and rested while there was time. Then it happened! Suddenly the hounds put the bruin on his feet and rolled with a roar into the north-side slopes of Reservoir Cove.

Reservoir Cove has characteristics quite different from its neighboring Little East Fork tributaries. It is steep to climb from start to finish and changes frequently from thickets to open woods. Halfway up its incline, big rocks become more than plentiful making a hunter's every step a cautious one. Walking or running in open rocky coves while following bear packs is risky business concerning the possibility of leg and knee injuries.

Reservoir Cove is located directly above the Daniel Boone Scout Camp and supplies it with sparking mountain fresh water. Its name is self-explanatory. Large water catching containers are found there to change the clear liquid from a long-lost resource into a precious commodity for the Boy Scout Camp found hundreds of yards below.

Camp Daniel Boone is a well-known location in Western North Carolina. It is tied to the Boy Scouts of America and is found up the Little East Fork of the Pigeon River at the end of the state-maintained road. Scouts from all over the Southern United States come there for retreats and outings of all descriptions. They receive outdoor training at Camp Daniel Boone along with enjoying a stay away from home.

In my opinion, Camp Daniel Boone is a very outstanding organization. The people that are affiliated and appointed to oversee the camp are precious to this day and time. Finding special people that will devote the time to teach leadership among our young ones of this time are more than scarce and are to be commended for their faithfulness.

Many times during my life, the folks at Camp Daniel Boone have taken the time to catch my dogs and then call to inform me of their whereabouts. The officials at the camp have gone out of their way on numerous occasions to accommodate hunters with lost-dog situations. Camp Daniel Boone is where most dogs will stop when coming out of the woods for the day.

In this photo Camp Daniel Boone sits upright for all to see. Numerous young scouts have been educated there and my hat is off to the folk that make the camp a success.

Bear hounds for the most part are very friendly animals and after coming in contact with young scouts will usually make themselves welcome. I commend the people of Camp Daniel Boone and thank them greatly for the years of friendship that has so freely been given to me.

I remember recognizing how my day had quickly changed from bad to better. As I ran the old trail as fast as possible, my legs started to give way because Bird Stand Ridge had taken a toll on my energy level. Stopping to listen at short intervals I began to wonder if I had enough stamina to head the fast moving pack off as they roared up Reservoir Cove.

To my surprise, the hounds suddenly slowed down to a crawling pace as I stopped briefly to listen again. Their barks seemed to shake the leaves on the trees and I could hear lots of yelping which made me aware of the fact that some dogs were definitely getting cut and bruised. After judging the distance between them and myself, I decided that I had sufficient time to make it through the big, rocky, hollow before they did.

Being unaware of the fact and to my astonishment, I found an old logging road that looked to be leading straight into the head of Reservoir Cove. It was a God send and I was then more than confident in getting to the loud pack before they crossed over onto the West Fork side of Fork Mountain.

The woods were damp that afternoon because of the overnight shower and that allowed me to move silently. At that time, I didn't know what was ahead of me for I couldn't recall ever being in that particular place in my life. The ground was covered in Ivy bushes where I was but at the snap of a finger, I stood in wide-open woods. The dogs were still below me and across a small ridge out of my sight. They sounded like a freight train as they roared up Reservoir Cove and I listened from the old road.

Could this possibly be my lucky day? That thought began to flash constantly through my mind as I hotfooted from one large rock to another in the upper most portion of Reservoir Cove. Not many feelings can compare with that of knowing the action is close. I had invested many steps that fall season into my hunting efforts and was long overdue a deserving shot.

The fracas had to end soon for I had never heard one that was any more complex. Serious things were happening at that point. I was astounded by all of the different noises coming from the next small hollow over from me. I could hear all sorts of growling from the short distance away.

My adrenaline level was pegged out during all of this and I was jumping at six-foot leaps. Subconsciously, I knew that running in the rocky cove was very dangerous but the twisted acoustic sounds made it worth chancing.

I remember thinking back again on how messed up the day had been from the start and could hardly believe it could end this easy. I knew that I was ahead of everybody else and suddenly realized that the moment of truth had finally come around for me.

The fall season had taken most of the leaves off of the huge Lynn trees there. I was aware of that factor and knew it had its advantages and disadvantages.

With no Ivy or Laurel bushes in the upper portion of Reservoir Cove, I could foresee problems if the dogs were by chance to tree in the wide-open woods. Slipping to the tree without being seen would be almost an accident. Shooting accurately from a longer distance than normal could be accomplished but with a greater chance of error.

Just as I figured to happen at any moment, the hounds started tree barking which was music to my ears. I carefully worked the lever on my Winchester injecting a live round into the chamber and started slipping toward them. After topping the last small rise I spotted the dogs springing from side to side of what looked to be a huge Lynn tree. My eyes moved up the trunk of the tree speedily and saw an animal that seemed to be bigger than I had anticipated. Black seemed to be spread over an unbelievable portion of the tree and I was surprised by its size.

I tried ever so hard to keep trees between the big beast and myself for shooting was out of the question from where I was. The distance was much too far and after looking the large trophy over, I didn't wish to take any chances if possible. As I slipped from one tree to the next, I discovered an opening in the timber about fifty yards from the pack and knew that it would be a sure giveaway of my presence.

At that point, I wasn't very confident of my next move or what it was to be for that matter as I stood behind the last tree between me and the vibrating hounds that were looking up with eagerness. Just in front of me on the opposite side of my natural blind was a huge flat rock about five feet in diameter with a height of approximately seven feet. I finally built enough nerve to ease out into the opening and sat down cautiously on the large boulder to position myself for sliding off of the other side.

As my body came to a sitting erect rest on the flat rock, the bear suddenly noticed me. I was afraid that would happen and even though I didn't want to I pulled my rifle slowly to my shoulder with little confidence. It started down the tree with small jumps paying the roaring pack little to no attention and I then made what my fellow hunters have many times called a lucky shot.

The excitement was almost more than I could bear. I couldn't seem to move across the rocky cove fast enough to get a closer look. Joy completely overtook me as I felt the thick fur on the outstanding animal and the dogs seemed to be prouder than I was. All I could do was pet the hounds vigorously and yell loudly. My mind was in a state that far outweighed any situation that I have ever been privileged to endure. Life had never offered anything better to me than what had just transpired in the last few minutes.

As I gradually started out of the unique trance, I thought about Chick and how proud he would be. I couldn't seem to get my hand-held radio out of my vest quick enough to see if the old timer would answer. When he did, I distinctly heard an emotion in his voice that I had never heard before.

He had moved from the West Fork side of Fork Mountain to the Camp Daniel Boone side and positioned himself to hear almost all of the heated race and realized that all he could do was depend on me.

His vocal sounds were shaken and scratchy and I could easily tell that his anxiety had gotten such a hold on him as to make him weep. Standing in the middle of the proud, joyous occasion, I felt so sorry for him in his handicapped condition and assured my friend to see him soon.

Within minutes the other hunters arrived and helped me celebrate the happy time. We had dogs that were hurt but after inspecting them carefully, found none of them to be life threatening. My father and I soon discussed the progress of the young dogs and recollected how many years it had been since we had hunted a talented pack of that caliber. It was evident and we concluded that our present pack was more competent in their hunting abilities than any we had ever owned.

For the next hour we sat around the tree to fellowship and relive parts of the confusing day--just four men and the dogs. It suddenly dawned on me how the smaller joys of life were sometimes the most meaningful. It was too good to be true and I expected to wake up at anytime and find out that I was only dreaming. My dad and I had spent quality time together that October Saturday and his optimistic lesson of faith to never give up was scribed into the pages of my mind forever.

CAUGHT BY SURPRISE

The wind blew and the rains came in sheets. Foul weather had entered the Western North Carolina region and played havoc on the third week of hunting season. The first significant cold front of autumn changed the beautiful October days into aggravating wet ones with noontime highs only in the mid forties.

It has always been a mystery to me how cold forty degrees can feel to a body that's been used to daytime highs at an average of seventy to eighty degrees for several months in a row. Early fall temperatures, after a warm, comfortable late summer feels like a single digit arctic blast. I looked forward to cooling weather after a hot summer in the fields but knowing that winter was for sure coming made me shiver from within.

While the low lands were only heavily dampened by rain, the highlands of the Cold Mountain Territory were frozen to a solid white and would give most anybody a chill looking from the Mundy Field Valley below. As a youngster, I can remember hunting with my father on Cold Mountain in weather conditions that we really had no business exposing our bodies to. I can recall several occasions when we experienced adverse, frozen precipitation while leading our hounds up and down Cold Mountain's ridges and coves.

I sometimes snicker to myself when I think back on the times my brother and I dealt with wet and iced clothing in the woods. As young lads at the ages on nine and thirteen, my brother and I would be astonished as we observed our pants legs being frozen solid from the bottom to just above our knees. They felt like stove pipes on our legs and the stiff, dead feeling was much of a serious thought for young boys while being pretty dog-gone comical also.

The frozen, snow covered woods of Western North Carolina makes for the most beautiful sight, but can be easily misleading to hunters and hikers concerning their personal safety.

In the present day, our party often engages in discussions concerning modern hunting and hiking apparel in which we are very privileged to have. The quality of clothing and footwear in the '60's and '70's couldn't come close to that of today.

In these days in which we live, getting caught in the high country thickets with wet feet and legs can mostly be blamed only on the hunter or hiker himself. Modernized field and stream outfits far outweigh the older ones and add high compatibility to the enjoyment of a good day in the woods.

The evening meal dishes bumped together making sleepy clanging sounds as we holed up in the snug den of the big log house. It was midweek and all of us had rested enough to be looking forward to the next hunting trip. Dad was to have no hunting fun until Saturday of that week because the day shift had colored his calendar through Friday evening. My brother and I laughed jokingly together as we explained how we would miss his presence the next day.

We talked with our hunting partners by telephone and a crowd of seven was at Frank's Country Store the next morning. We were to take a potluck trip that day not asking for a lot just a runnable track as usual. The Little East Fork of the Pigeon was on our agenda but we were to roam the left side that hazy Thursday instead of the right.

The left side of the Little East Fork was our choice that morning because of its south-side layout making it by far the warmest. That factor was important to us for the highly elevated ridge tops of Cold Mountain were to be frozen over with a thick layer of cold fog.

On the south side, the sun could participate in a hasty meltdown not to mention giving us a better chance to warm our bodies periodically along the way. The weather was much different than it had been in the previous two weeks. Staying warm was then to be our problem versus the stopping at intervals to cool off in which we had done just a few days back.

Four big coves in general make up the left side of the Little East Fork and in past years have treated me to many good days in the woods as I hiked and hunted my way through them. The first substantial cove on the left side of the Little East Fork creek is known as Panther Branch.

Panthers are now extinct in Western North Carolina but as I researched how Panther Branch was named I discovered that they were plentiful in the early nineteen hundreds. Several old hands from different communities of Western North Carolina have assured me of the panther's presence in those days and described their squelching yelps to be hair standing especially at night. I've heard older folks on many occasions speak of how something or someone squealed like a panther. I guess that old saying is a bit more than just a figure of speech.

The bigger portion of Panther Branch is privately owned. Mr. and Mrs. H. D. Fishback are among those who reside in Panther Branch after choosing to make their home in the mountains of Western North Carolina in 1975. They have caught lost dogs on several occasions and have always promptly called by telephone to inform our party of their whereabouts. H. D. and his wife are top quality people and have been neighborly toward our party down through the years. We all appreciate them greatly.

The next cove above Panther Branch is called Schoolhouse Branch. Schoolhouse Branch is a beautiful place and compares quite equal to Panther Branch in size. Nestled quietly in the lower portion of Schoolhouse Branch is the Laurel Grove Baptist Church. The church looks much like a perfect picture from a storybook of most unique places. A schoolhouse stood where the building is now until 1930 when it was converted to a church. Since then it has undergone modern renovations and enhances the countryside around it.

Seen here is a portion of Panther Branch. It is hidden from most angles and is a much bigger piece of woodland than most folks realize.

The upper half of Schoolhouse Branch has several old logging roads through it but are gated and closed to vehicle travel. Bears while running from dogs hardly ever make their way toward Schoolhouse Branch but when they do, will scarcely take a tree or bay up for any length of time before entering the Panther Branch or Dix Creek areas. After several hard hours of running, tired dogs will fall out of a race in Schoolhouse Branch especially if they by chance remember the friendly people who live in the valley below.

Frank, Paul and Clay Woody along with several of their family members live at the mouth of Schoolhouse Branch. These three men are brothers. All of their homes are in yelling distance of each other and sit on one of the most picture perfect places of the West Fork of the Pigeon River. The Woodys are top-quality people also and have always made the hunting party and me welcome.

They're also well known for their Christian way of living and have possibly gone out of their way to show true southern hospitality when most folk would have been bent to the breaking point of aggravation.

Many times they have been awakened in the middle of the night by lost hunting dogs wandering about their residences. Instead of becoming mad, they get up to tie the lost hound and feed it before calling his or her master the next morning. The Woodys know how much I appreciate them and they are an overwhelming asset to the Little East Fork community.

On up the line, the next cove above Schoolhouse Branch is known as Murray Cove. Murray Cove is a piney, hardwood mixed hollow in which logging roads are plentiful also. In the mid-1900's Murray Cove and Schoolhouse Branch were logged together. Looking down on both of these coves from high above on the Dix Creek Top Trail has made me wonder many times how many logs were harvested off of these areas then.

The Laurel Grove Baptist Church seen in this picture makes for one of the most beautiful scenes in the Southeastern United States. This reverent structure adds a surge of character to the Little East Fork community.

Frank, Paul and Clay Woody--friends for life

In the upper portion of Murray Cove on the southern most slopes finds an open pasture called Rickman's field. It is the divider between Murray Cove and the biggest and last cove to the left of the Little East Fork named Sorrell's Creek.

Sorrell's Creek is a vast exceptional work of art in which our Creator assembled with great pride. The enjoyment of Sorrell's Creek has been a giant factor in my outdoor experiences since childhood.

Its gushing clear creek has produced many Mountain Speckled Trout over the years and I still remember the fun days I've spent in Sorrell's Creek as a youngster with my father. That time together is a valuable gem in my life for Sorrell's Creek is where he put a fly rod in my hands for the first time.

On numerous occasions, we fished there and then cooked our lunch over an open fire. Those meals were of the best I've ever eaten. I can still smell the appetizing aroma of fresh boiling coffee bubbling by the flames mixed with the irresistible smell of streaked side meat sizzling in the old black iron skillet. I consider myself very blessed to have experienced such a childhood environment and hope to enjoy even more springtime days on the creek bank with him.

Found on the left side of Sorrell's Creek is a rough, sharp edged ridge that hunters know as Piney. This ridge stands out dramatically when viewing the south side of Sorrell's Creek. For some unknown reason, a small boundary of pine trees grow there amidst acres and acres of hardwoods. Piney is thick with underbrush and is of rugged terrain making it perfect for bears. We had chosen to take the pack up Piney at least part of the way hoping to find runnable scent.

Sorrell's Creek, the place where my childhood teachings of the great outdoors were first administered.

At that time, there was a slightly usable trail up Piney but it didn't wind back and forth like most of the paths in the Cold Mountain area. The trail angled more or less straight up. It was grown over with brush but was still somewhat useful even when leading dogs. Since then, the quality of the Piney Trail has declined so much as to hardly find it much less stay on it for any length of time. The trail was steep but climbing was unusually easy that morning for the cold twenty-degree weather seem to manufacture extra oxygen for us as we gave our pulmonary system another workout.

Halfway up Piney we stopped for a rest and hadn't found anything to put our hounds on. The usual steam was streaming up from our clothes as we leaned our backs against trees on the steep slope to rest.

We were operating that morning without a distinct plan but subconsciously knew that the young pack was more or less made and the pressure was off of us making our party worry free. We were in the click so to speak and lately it seemed that we could do nothing wrong.

When we regained full strength we finally decided that it was time to come up with a successful strategy for our midweek adventure. We had stopped in sight of open woods that led toward the upper portions of Murray Cove and Schoolhouse Branch and we were tempted to take the pack through them as to make dog leading much easier.

My brother made us a deal that we couldn't turn down when he offered to take the young strike dog straight up the last part of the rough butt on Piney while we took the pack around to the elevated Dix Creek Top. Before parting ways, we agreed to communicate by radio at fifteen-minute intervals and we were off.

The clear open woods made for good walking and the party seemed to enjoy leading the dogs toward the high top. Just after radioing my brother for the second time, we reached our temporary destination to find the wind gusting at thirty or forty miles per hour. He had reported to us that they had found no scent whatsoever and for us to stay put on the ledge above him until further conversation.

Our bodies began to cool after twenty long minutes and we became too cold for comfort. Hearing anything significant was almost impossible for the howling winds made loud rustling noises in the freshly fallen leaves.

Twenty more minutes went strangely by and besides being frozen to the bone, we were starting to get concerned because we hadn't heard anything else from my big brother.

Hand-held walkie-talkies have been blasphemed for as long as I can remember concerning their use in hunting activities. I couldn't disagree more. Even though hand-held radios make for easier communication with fellow hunters their disadvantages far outweigh their advantages.

The old-time hunters had a much better success rate without them. That is simply a fact. Hand-held radios can be heard by wild animals at an enormous distance, therefore making them easily aware of human presence.

While having poor eyesight, black bears have very keen senses of hearing and smelling. When walkie-talkies are operated at the wrong time during a hunt, bears, while running from dogs will immediately change their direction to detour them.

Hand-held radios are aggravating to the elder hunters in the party. They claim that many races have been long winded on their behalf. Before 1960, bear hunters communicated in a much different way. They hooted like an owl or whistled like a bird from one ridge top to the next. One of these old timers is Mr. John Lambert who I admire for his unreal stamina.

John Lambert has probably been involved with and heard more bear races than any man still living in the Western North Carolina Mountains. John is a son of my grandfather's sister. He was born on Cooper's Creek in the Cherokee area of Western North Carolina in 1905. He still resides in the Cherokee community.

His personality is that of extreme friendliness. The kids love to be around John for he can tell stories as to make a person feel like they're by his side the whole way.

John amazes me when I watch him move around. He often makes me wonder how he does it and I sometimes try to imagine my mobility skills when and if I reach his age. He is a fine cook and is well known for his delicious pound cakes. John is a true legend of his time and my respect for him is that of enormous stature.

More time had elapsed and my hunting partners and I were getting extremely cold. The dogs shook as to warm themselves and I started seriously wondering what was going on with my brother. At a point of taking no more misery, one of the hunters responded that his batteries may have been weak and decided to walk back to the top of the last ridge we had crossed to maybe get in closer radio range of him. Just as he went out of sight, our hounds suddenly stood on their back feet and reared to go with barks of excitement.

Some kind of predator had come so close to us that its scent evidently filled the air and the dogs were getting more apprehensive by the second. I remember how we discussed yellingly about what we should do and quickly came to the conclusion that it must be a bear. We decided to unsnap all of them and when we did the woods rang with noises of all calibers and the race was on.

The unusual predicament that we had experienced that morning happens few and far between. I have mentioned in a previous chapter of how turning all of the hounds loose at the same time almost always makes for a sure failure but there are exceptions once in a while. When a bear, for whatever reason, has been jumped and unknowingly makes it way towards a hunting pack, the scent becomes suddenly strong making the dogs go out of control.   When this happens, the only alternative is to loosen them immediately.

John Lambert, a legend of his time

Deep blue sky lay over the Cold Mountain Range ridges and coves and even though the temperatures were low, the bright sunlight colored the scene with beauty. The pack faded through Schoolhouse Branch and into Panther Branch with a blast and was out of our hearing in a flash. All of this mess had happened in a few minutes and my mind was blown with excitement.

I was dimly aware of my brother's presence and subconsciously knowing that something was wrong, I knew that he was all right and decided to follow the pack. In the midst of my wild thoughts, another wave of worry washed over me. The pack had entered Panther Branch with a stinging speed and I figured that they wouldn't stop there for long. Trying to counter their next move was the problem at hand.

I distinctly remember a fine hunting partner being by my side that cold morning and I often laugh to myself when I think back about two big young men bouncing down the Dix Creek Top Trail with ground-jarring leaps. Both of us weighed over two hundred pounds at the time and he was quite a shot taller and heavier than I was.

His name is Julian Buchanan. We all called him by his nickname, Mackey. Mackey comes from a family made up of a big strong type of people. He weighs at least two hundred fifty pounds and stands six foot, three inches tall.

His hair is of extreme darkness coupled with brown eyes and he speaks with words of seriousness most of the time. For his size, Mackey is as tough in the woods as ever could be found when it comes to hunting from daylight until late evening. All-day trips mean nothing to him for his strength holds out unbelievably. He likes any kind of hunting with dogs and enjoys the sport of bear hunting with a great passion.

Mackey served his time in the U.S. Military and took a bride while stationed in Germany. I've sat in the woods on many occasions and listened inquisitively to him describe Germany's scenery very adjectivally. He has explained to me lots of times how the geographical layout in Germany was much like that of Western North Carolina.

Mackey Buchanan, a faithful man who is always willing.

It has also impressed me down through the years to acquire knowledge of German cooking from Mackey. Some of the mouth-watering recipes that he describes while on the trail hunting makes a man reach deeper into his vest pockets to see what's left to eat.

I've considered it a pleasure to have spent many years in the woods with a fine hunting partner such as Mackey. He's been devoted to the sport and that's what it takes to be successful.

Mackey and I bounced heavily toward a well-known point on the Dix Creek Top Trail called the Bus. Hunters of old camped in a bus body at this particular location. As a youngster I can remember the rusty bus body interesting me as we passed it during hunting trips. It sat on the lower side of the trail and was held up by locust posts. Over time it has deteriorated and 30 to 40 years of falling leaves have almost camouflaged it permanently. Even though a few parts of the old bus are all that is still visible, our entire hunting party knows where to go when it is mentioned.

It puts my mind in awe when I begin to think of how the points included in the Cold Mountain Territory were named. During years of research concerning them, I have learned the story of most but several of them are still a mystery. The majority of ridges and coves have carried the same names for hundreds of years I suppose.

About one hundred yards from the bus, Mackey and I heard the pack cross the Dix Creek ridge below us as they delivered themselves out of Panther Branch and into Dix Creek. We didn't have a lot of time to waste as we discussed our next move for the dogs were moving like the wind and were close together making them roar like a train.

The bear seemed to be destined for Lenior Creek as most of them do in that area which meant that the dogs were to cross a ridge that Mackey and I were running most diligently toward called Brushy.

Brushy Ridge is the dividing ridge between the two upper most coves in Dix Creek. It was named properly because its dense thickets definitely fit the old timer's description as being too thick to blow smoke through. At least one whole chapter could be written concerning Brushy Ridge and the trail up it is my favorite of all the trails included in the Cold Mountain area.

Many good days have been started and ended on Brushy and I can't imagine how many times that I've been up and down it. The construction of the Brushy Ridge Trail is much like something that few people have ever seen. Several places along its steep grade look to have been carved through the granite rock. The men of old that performed this superior building task of the Brushy Ridge Trail went home in late evening with extremely tired bodies I'm sure.

The sound of the pack was completely out of Panther Branch when Mackey and I went by the bus. At that time I seriously doubted us to reach where we needed to be on time. The part of the Brushy Ridge Trail in which we were traveling is flat and easy going. Although we were moving faster than the noisy pack, our chances of getting down the steep rocky portion of the trail to become even with them was slim to none.

The Brushy Ridge Trail changes from flat ground to a sharply angled rocky terrain in a distance less than one hundred and fifty feet. Between the two changes lies a most peaceful point on the Brushy Ridge Trail that we hunters call the Horse Barn.

At this location, a small bubbling stream trickles slowly through a bed of rock. The small stream never changes even in dry conditions. It makes little to no sound as it progresses its way across the trail and by its presence a hunter's thirst can be quenched with clean mountain spring water that is of extremely high clarity. Our club members freely fill water bottles as they pass the small brook for the next available water is far away when destined for the Cold Mountain Swag.

The rocky Brushy Ridge Trail in this picture stands in my mind as a keepsake. I have been blessed to walk it many times and enjoy just being there.

In a small flat about fifty feet west of the small stream is the location in which the Horse Barn was erected. Earl Gibson who was a life-long resident of Dix Creek owned a large tract of land in the upper Dix Creek area and made his living from logging timber. He logged virtually the entire head of Dix Creek and was solely responsible for the Horse Barn's existence on Brushy Ridge.

Earl would often feed and water his team of horses after work hours and stable them in the small barn before leaving on foot for home thus taking a great deal of stress from them by saving their energy for the next day's work.

He said that a person had to take good care of a team in those days for they were responsible for a man's living. Earl said that modern day dozers and log skidders could be refueled and work right on but horses had to be fed properly and rested in a dry structure at night if a man was to receive top-quality work from them the next day.

Only the bottom most timbers of the barn are still visible and I think of Earl every time I pass by them. The small two-horse barn was approximately one and a half miles from his house and the trail to it was uphill for him all the way. I often wonder how many folk would survive in this day if they had to make wages in the same manner in which Earl did.

Just before reaching the Horse Barn, Mackey and I noticed that the dogs had suddenly halted. They sounded to be treed but I found that hard to believe because I had never known a pack of hounds to stop a bear for any length of time there. We waited for a minute or two expecting them to move again and to our surprise they stayed put.

It was decision time again and Mackey and I whispered a plan as to what we thought might work the best.

We wondered where the other hunters were because none of them were in sight behind us. I quickly suggested to Mackey that he should go back the way we had come two or three hundred feet and drop straight down on the stopped pack while I hustled down the Brushy Ridge Trail to position myself at equal elevation to them.

I knew by the look in Mackey's eye that he understood the fast-made plans. If the pack started to move again I would be waiting in their projected path, therefore, all of our eggs weren't in the same basket--so to speak.

Mackey seemed proud when we parted ways and as I observed his eager steps over my shoulder, I knew that he was determined from within. I ran making as little noise as possible by the Horse Barn.

The small stones rolled under my feet as I started down the steeply graded midsection of the Brushy Ridge Trail but I maintained the same speed anyway. I lost elevation in a heartbeat and my body was shaken severely from running on the rocky ground. My knees were aching from holding back down the steep grade and my breath was short.

The land on Brushy Ridge is covered with Mountain Ivy and finding a clearing to provide accurate shooting was almost impossible. I frantically searched for a break in the dense thicket that was big enough to maybe get a quick shot if need be. I finally satisfied myself and sat down quietly on the lower bank of the old trail and waiting impatiently for the pack to either start my way or to hear Mackey sound off.

In a way I didn't look forward to the ring from Mackey's rifle for he carried what most of us called a small cannon. Mackey's bear gun is a .444 Marlin. It consists of a caliber literally the size of an average little finger. There's no mistaking its distinct sound if in decent hearing distance of it.

His rifle not only makes an unforgettable blast but is also the heaviest gun that I've ever known a bear hunter to carry. It's not unusual while bear hunting for a man to sometimes walk up to twelve or fifteen miles in a day's time. Mackey has carried his .444 for as long as I can remember. Sometimes I wonder how he manages but he seems to do it with little to no problem.

I rested reverently thinking of how blessed I was to have experienced such a gallant morning. As I waiting for something to transpire, I couldn't help but realize how lucky a person was to be healthy and strong enough to enjoy such a sport as ours. I thought of my mom teaching us boys as youngsters that out of all the treasures in life, good health is the best gift of all. I can recall her saying, "Poor people in good health are far better off than wealthy sick folk."

Thinking about those things in which Mom had endeavored to teach us boys suddenly made me wonder where my brother was. It puzzled me. What could have happened to him was heavy on my mind. I knew I had distinctly heard the young strike dog's voice that my brother had with him when the fracas broke loose but not hearing from him was getting worrisome for me.

The sky had turned to a deeper shade of blue and the patchy fog had begun to lift off of Brushy. Most of the trees on the south-side slopes of the Cold Mountain area had shed at least half of their leaves but the ones on Brushy Ridge had held on a bit longer. Its extreme north-side location was responsible for that I'm sure and the sight that I watched come into view beneath the rising fog was spectacular. The bright colors from the oaks, maples and poplars were of the prettiest pastels.

In fall, the deciduous trees of Western North Carolina turn the carbohydrates in their leaves into sugars and start moving them from the twigs and buds down into their roots for storage. Leaf cells then break down starting with the chloroplasts, which contain green pigment chlorophyll. In turn, this process reveals the beautiful reds, yellows, and oranges that were in the leaves all along but hidden through the summer months under green. The autumn colors that I observed that morning as I waited were some of the finest my eyes had ever beheld.

It was somewhat of a different experience for me to sit still and depend upon someone else's hunting intelligence but thinking back on Mackey's determined face made me rest much easier. Eight or ten more minutes went slowly by and the hounds were barking louder than ever. Nerves were at a usual high and something needed to happen for my curiosity was getting the best of me.

Mackey's .444 finally rang with a giant blast that echoed for a good fifteen or twenty seconds. I snickered to myself before even getting up from my comfortable trail-side seat as I imagined Mackey's excitement. Then I yelled as loud as I could with words of "Yes" "Yes." I heard Mackey distantly yell back and I knew that it was over and hurriedly commenced on a grade through the thick rocky cove toward him.

It took me about fifteen minutes to reach him and I noticed his big smile from at least seventy yards. He had performed his job well. The dogs weren't treed but rather bayed up between huge rocks making shooting very difficult for Mackey. He was commended plentifully and as we relived the morning together, I noticed one of our fellow hunters, whom I have always considered to be my little brother, barreling down the steep mountainside toward us.

The fall colors, as could be imagined in this picture combine themselves perfectly to assemble a great masterpiece given so freely by the mountains of Western North Carolina.

His name is Scott Blaylock. We all called him by his nickname "Red" which is self-explanatory. Red's hair matches his name to a tee and his complexion is light. Red and I go back many years. We've been close friends since childhood and he took up the sport of bear hunting because he resided on the farm with our family much of his younger days.

Red has always been fast on foot and holds up well in long race situations. He also has an unbelievable sense of humor and can make a joke on most any occasion. Red adds a special zip to every hunting trip with his keen chuckle of laughter and as we celebrated with Mackey, our friendship was certainly at a life-long high. He was and still is an outstanding asset to our party.

The three of us enjoyed being together during the next half-hour and were on top of the world. We couldn't have been happier. All of the money on earth couldn't buy the fellowship that we enjoyed there on Brushy and as the dogs finally began to quieten we heard a distant yell high above us toward the Dix Creek top.

We chuckled loudly after hearing the far off shout. The excitement had been so great that we had temporarily forgotten my big brother. We knew by the tone of the voice that it was his and was relieved by that. At the time we didn't realize that he wasn't aware that the hunt had ended and as we listened more closely, we heard him yelling out questions pertaining to the present location of the pack.

The three of us really got a kick of humor then and after laughing until our stomachs hurt, we finally got enough breath back in our chests to shout back at him to come downhill toward us because the race was over. We couldn't seem to stop laughing and we rolled in the freshly fallen leaves until we hurt.

Scotty Blaylock, the man who will always be a little brother
that I did not have.

Even today, I can still remember my brother's forlorn look as he progressed his way into sight on that brisk midday. He stumbled up and took a good look at the fine two hundred pound bear and silently stood still nodding his head up and down slowly in disgust. "That's him," he said, and fell to the ground back first as we laughed even more.

At last, he got around to telling us what had happened to him after we had separated. He and the young strike dog had jumped the bear while slipping quietly up Piney but with a malfunctioned radio he had no choice but to turn young Timber loose solo and hope that we would hear him.

We then gladly told him in full detail, as Paul Harvey would say, "the rest of the story." He enjoyed every second and after nothing else could be said we started descending the rocky cove toward civilization on Dix Creek.

Chick was waiting of course to give us a much-needed ride and was happy to see each of us. As we rode down the rough road in the back of his truck, Red and I still laughed every time we looked at each other. My brother Mark noticed our silly actions and pointed his finger as to insinuate that enough was enough.

The chores on the farm were enjoyable that evening and every chance we received, a good word was thrown in concerning the fine pack of hounds we had been privileged to train.

Lady luck was on our side of late and the fall season in which we had experienced so far seemed to be throwing every ball straight down the middle—even when taken by surprise.

MYSTERY STEW

The fire popped and cracked as the flames majestically wrapped around the backside of small fore stick of hickory wood in the warm basement fireplace. My brother and I sat quietly in front of it watching the embers glow, along with enjoying their cozy heat and sipping Mom's Russian tea, cup by cup.

It used to be that people sat around a fire and enjoyed being with each other, making family listening and speaking top priority for a good evening of entertainment. The memories of that are grand to me and my brother and I trimmed out the day by reliving parts of it--especially Mackey's happiness.

Now days, I can't help but believe that a great portion of quality, evening family time is gone. For the most part, I guess sitting together by open flames of a fireplace during the night hours as a family is too. Houses, after work hours aren't quiet and peaceful anymore but are much the opposite in many residences. The same quiet old houses are now full of television sets, washers, dryers and in many cases animals and a great deal of noise.

Oh well, times change, I suppose but I'm not so sure that they always change for the better. I know I certainly seemed to enjoy the peaceful nights at home by the fire whether it be at our house or one of the close neighbors.

The nearest house to ours at that particular time was my dad's brother, Glenn Griffin. I always called him Uncle Glenn and was awfully fond of him. He was a big man dressed in overalls for any occasion and loved us boys like his own. Uncle Glenn was constantly joking with us and all

of the kids in the cove were astonished at the different
abilities he performed with only one hand and two fingers.

Glenn Griffin, a skilled mason and a person that never met a
stranger.

My Uncle Glenn had experienced a life-threatening accident as a young man. While crossing a fence with a loaded shotgun he fell allowing the gun's hammer to contact one of the wooden fence rails causing it to go off unwontedly. This accident cost him three fingers on his left hand but also left a sizable amount of lead shot in his chest cavity. He was down for an extended period but finally regained his strength fully. Uncle Glenn was a rock mason by trade. This was his up-most way of making a living accompanied by farming an average tobacco allotment and raising a few cattle. He suffered in the summertime's hot sunlight as he laid rocks but enjoyed his trade immensely.

All of his work still stands unfaultered today. Several substantial jobs that he conquered are eye catchers to people as they pass by them on a daily basis. Two of these jobs are located in the city limits of Canton, North Carolina, one of which is on Pennsylvania Avenue near the Canton Library while the other is a large portion of the Canton Nursing Home that he so diligently veneered.

Uncle Glenn also built many chimneys and rock walls throughout Haywood County and built a retaining wall behind the Mount Zion Baptist Church on Dix Creek that is simply crafty to say the least.

He enjoyed his work and took great pride in it but he also had an untamed passion for the sport of bear hunting. When I became a teenager, Uncle Glenn had become too old to make the initial drive but was always willing to stand a gap hoping to get in on some action. He's passed on to the next life now but his memories bring good thoughts to me as I recollect my younger years of life. Isn't that all any of us could ask for whenever we leave this world?

The work of art seen here was built by my Uncle Glenn in the city limits of Canton, North Carolina.

This photograph shows another crafty piece of work that he so patiently built one day at a time.

Sometimes I would walk up the hill to Uncle Glenn's house after supper to sit in his modest kitchen in a straight chair by the warm cook stove and listen to his stories of excitement. Whether they were about hunting, farming or working made no difference for he had a way of making any story interesting.

Friday's rest was much needed and besides that, Dad worked off on that evening to start a two-week vacation to end the hunting season. Mark and I felt confident to go hunting without Dad but were much more satisfied when he was along. We depended on him a little too much at times but then again, "what's a Dad for?" The three of us were close knitted and we decided not to go back to the woods until Saturday as we could be accompanied by his presence.

As a hunting party, we usually took at least two trips a year through the highest elevated portion of Cold Mountain to try our luck at dogging a blackie. The high country ridges and coves of Cold Mountain are some of the most rugged ones found in the Western North Carolina region and that is simply a fact.

For some reason, that particular portion of Cold Mountain seems to be the favorite pick of my father. He strictly loves to hunt the high ridges of Lenior Creek, Big Anderson Creek and the upper most parts of Cold Creek.

These locations are hard to hike and hunt because the trail quality to them is poor besides being very remote from vehicles. To hunt these parts of Cold Mountain a person has two to three hours of steady pulling and reaching them with energy to spare is definitely a challenge for any man. None the less, that idea was on his mind heavily and looked to be the plan for Saturday of the third week of hunting season, starting one to two hours before daybreak.

I lay in bed on Friday night thinking about the long hard pull that was on tap for the next morning but looked forward to spending time there with my family. I tried to imagine what kind of story could be written in a diary when the time came to go back to bed. The curiosity finally wore off and I slipped into a deep sleep.

I woke to the sound of frying pans clanging together and the noise made me realize how hungry I was. A country breakfast aroma eased up the long stairwell to my and my brother's bedrooms. The bacon smell made us jerk our clothes on frantically and we couldn't seem to get ourselves down the steps to the table full of food quick enough.

After breakfast the three of us sat in the basement lacing our boots tightly knowing that the pieces of cowhide leather was going to take a beating in the next six to eight hours. When our vests were packed with biscuits for a mid morning brunch, we were out the door to the dog lot.

What happened in the next few minutes will haunt my memory forever. I always took care of loading Sailor when we were going hunting and what I found when I stumbled up to the front of his warmly straw-bedded box was depressing and discouraging. Sailor was hard to wake and slowly turned his head toward me when I spoke.

His eyes were heavily mattered and his slow groans informed me that he wasn't able to endeavor what life had to offer him that morning. I tugged gently on his chain and as his collar tightened on the wrinkled skin he stretched his sore neck toward me as to be ashamed of his age. He shut his eyes when I slacked the chain and laid his head down on his paws to confirm his incapabilities.

All of this really tore me up emotionally and I tried to explain Sailor's situation to my dad as he loaded the other hounds. I was relieved when he said, "Well boys, let's just leave him here today and let him rest." I quickly had bad feelings about the day from its rocky start. Knowing that Sailor wasn't in the line up sent sounds of doubt through my mind. That was the first time I could ever remember leaving him at home while we went hunting but climbed into the truck with a determined attitude anyway and decided to make the best of it. Hunting without Sailor was a problem that would surely be difficult to overcome but we had it to do.

The trip my dad had planned for that Saturday had evidently made some of the hunters doubt their stamina because a head count of five was all I can remember that showed up. The high country hills of Cold Mountain is one of the absolute hardest climbs in Sherwood Forest and has a way of making people find excuses to be involved in other activities on certain occasions.

Nevertheless, my dad, my brother and me started our walk with the dogs about 5:45 a.m. from the small vehicle turnaround at Brushy Ridge on Dix Creek. As mentioned previously Brushy is a steep one for the first forty to fifty minutes and is ideal for making a body catch his second wind.

The walk was enjoyable up Brushy that morning for the weather was of clear skies with no wind and the temperatures had moderated overnight to a comfortable fifty degrees. Walking behind my dad had always been enjoyable anyway because he stays at a steady pace instead of fast and slow thus making a person less apt to fight the steep climb.

We drank plenty of good sparkling water at the Horse Barn and made our way talkatively on toward the Dix Creek Top Trail as we had done so many times. In about one hour we arrived at the Cold Mountain Swag and had found no track to put our hound's noses in.

The sun had just beamed through the oak laps on the eastern horizon and made a beautiful site for any man to see. The sky was of a deepest blue and the distant ridge tops were lined with a trace of orange and played a significant role in the early sunrise that day.

I felt young that morning and it seemed by his actions that Dad did too. I have always been happiest when I knew that he was happy and my brother and I were enjoying

125

fellowship with our father that morning that now days is almost obsolete in many people's lives. He acted to be feeling as young as us boys and that had a particular way of letting us know that we were in for a day of fun.

The Cold Mountain Swag was most beautiful that morning when we arrived there just after sunrise. In fact, the grassy fields were too comfortable looking to pass up so we took a few minutes to sit down and enjoy the rays and have a snack.

It's fun to watch the dogs' reactions when food is taken out of vest pockets. They suddenly become interested in that rather than hunting and after they beg intensely for so long we usually give them a portion of whatever we're partaking of. Bear dogs normally have a healthy appetite and it matters not to them what it is as long as its edible. Most hounds will eat anything from crackers to potato chips and in most cases will eat any kind of candy. We got quite a kick out of their actions as we were stopped in the swag and then proceeded on the trail toward the high top of Cold Mountain.

There is a small-unmarked path that intersects with the high top Cold Mountain Trail known as the Plane Crash Trail. Very few people are aware of it and a person that is not very familiar with the area could never find it. The Plane Crash Trail was established by hunters many years ago. It is a short cut to Old Bald Gap that is located on the dividing ridge between the head of Lenior Creek and the head of Cold Creek. Hunters use this trail to grade the mountain in an even cut rather than climbing all the way to the top of Cold Mountain and then out the ledge to where the point of the Old Bald Ridge and the Cold Mountain Lead come together. It is much faster and much more simple for a hunter especially if his energy levels are running low.

We made our way up the Cold Mountain Trail onto the Plane Crash Trail with no problem and entered a sharp little cove that could tell a most horrifying story if it could by chance talk. Every time I walk through it, a mysterious feeling comes over me that's unexplainable. On each occasion, I subconsciously imagine a most traumatic experience that transpired there so many years ago.

On Friday, September 13, 1946, a B-25 Bomber plane piloted by General Paul B. Wurtsmith crashed into the side of the very highest peak of Cold Mountain in which there were no survivors. Five men were aboard the B-25 and were in flight from Selfridge, Michigian, to Tampa, Florida. It was a most traumatic time from what I can gather and several people of the Bethel and Cruso communities were involved in the rescue effort.

Most of the wreckage was airlifted off of Cold Mountain by helicopter and to my understanding is presently on display at a military base in Oscoda, Michigan. This base was named in memory of General Wurtsmith and is attributed to that foggy night of long ago.

Hindsight is, of course, always 20/20. But, I have stood at the crash sight on many occasions and observed how close the aircraft came to clearing the high mountain peak. The old saying that an inch is as good as a mile certainly would have held true in that situation. If the plane had been one hundred feet higher in elevation or if it had been one hundred yards to the right or left it would have cleared the rugged mountainside with no problem whatsoever.

The timber there shows no signs of the crash to this day. Even though the hot blast of fuel killed all of the trees there on sight, second growth has occurred since making it absolutely unnoticeable.

When looking at the high top of Cold Mountain from the Cruso Valley, there is a scarred place that looks to be a narrow strip of barren land measuring approximately one hundred feet wide and one hundred and fifty yards long. Many folk that have never been there think that this is where the plane crashed and blew down the steep sidling ground but I can confirm that this is not true. The bare score there is one cove to the West from the original crash sight and is nothing more than a common slide caused from a narrow strip of very rocky faulty ground.

Although ninety percent of the wreckage was removed, there are still some visible parts there. Years of falling leaves have hidden most of the pieces that were left behind but some are still visible even today. As a youngster, I can remember, a large portion of the cockpit that was still intact enough to tell what it was and my brother and I were very interested in its presence. Since then it has also been removed.

I suppose there is a substantial amount of sentiment built into each of us as human beings but I have treasured a small piece of the plane since I was ten years old. While hunting with my father, I found a small piece of riveted aluminum and as a keepsake carried it out of the woods to home. I've carried a small piece of the metal in my hunting vest down through the years as a sentimental keepsake. I'm not sure that I'm a believer of luck, but for some reason I find myself a lot more comfortable knowing that it's in my pocket.

We light footed on past the crash site toward Old Bald Gap as we hunters call it. This particular point is where the Plane Crash Trail and the Old Bald Trail intersect. There's nothing special to be written about Old Bald Gap but down the grown-over Old Bald Trail about one hundred

yards is located a special piece of scenery that means a great
deal to me known as Old Bald.

ENTERPRISE

Greatest Pulp and Paper Town ⋅ 14 Pages

THURSDAY, SEPTEMBER 19, 1946 $2.00 PER YEAR—SINGLE COPY 5c

FIVE PERISH IN CRASH—Here is where five bodies were recovered late Sunday from the wreckage of a B-25 which crashed into Cold mountain in the Pisgah area. Friday. Among the dead was Maj-Gen. Paul B. Wurtsmith, temporary commander of the Eighth Air Force.—Photo by John Anderson, Brevard.

SEARCHERS FAIL TO LOCATE PLANE LOST SINCE 1944

Army Party Gave Up Hunt Near Maggie Fri

Failing to locate the main wreckage of the Army Green plane, lost since 1944, Army men searching party abandoned the ground hunt Friday and returned to the Greenville air base that afternoon.

The search was renewed last week after pieces of a wing was

Five Killed When Bomber Crashed On Cold Mountain In Pisgah Area Friday

Bodies Recovered From Wreckage Sunday

Five persons were killed, including Major General Paul B Wurtsmith, temporary commander of the Eighth Air Force, when a B-25 bomber crashed into Cold Mountain Friday afternoon.

More than fifty planes soared above the mountain peaks between Asheville and Bristol Saturday in search of the missing bomber, on flight from Selfridge field, Mich.,

Seen here is the newspaper clipping from that gloomy September
in 1946 describing the traumatic plane crash.

Old Bald is part of the ridge that separates the upper portions of Cold Creek and Lenior Creek and is simply no more than a cluster of tall gray granite rocks sticking out of the ground at an approximate twenty feet height. The view from the rocks of Old Bald on a clear, blue day is that of extraordinary quality.

The distant hollows and ridges look as if a small arm's length could touch them from the comfortable seat that a person can enjoy there. The rocks are bench shaped in several different places and comes in handy for the entire party to gather when listening for dogs.

Sitting peacefully that morning on the rocks of Old Bald, my dad suggested to Mark and me an idea in which I thought little of. It was his prerogative, since we hadn't found any bear scent to put our hounds down on, to turn them loose and let them hunt a bear on their own. Dad's brain storm almost put my brother and me into a frantic fit and after watching our father laugh for several minutes at our frowning facial expressions, we did decide to at least hear his explanation out.

He said, "Boys, don't get so alarmed. Your grandpa and me used to hunt our dogs loose quite often. Let them do the work," he said. He then went on to say that well-trained dogs running loose through the woods was much better than fifteen inexperienced ones on a leash. He then told my brother and I something that I've looked back on many times and until this day can still hear him saying.

"Listen," he said, "you al' probably don't realize this, but were privileged today to be hunting with the best pack we've ever had together. You guys will no doubt live the rest of your lives never being fortunate enough to have this many number one dogs at a single time. "Trust them," he said, "They're to that point now."

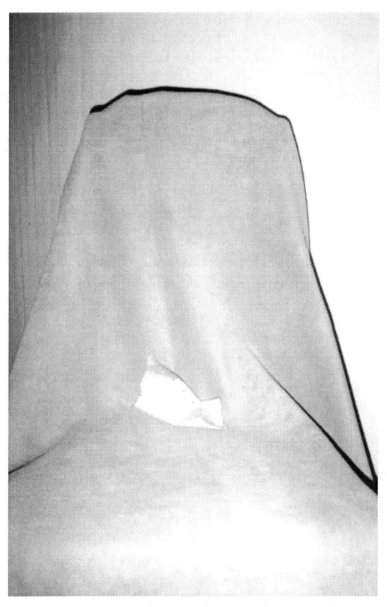

Pictured here is the small piece of riveted aluminum left behind from the crash of 1946 that I have treasured since childhood.

We sat silently after his serious statements and we watched him slowly unsnap Timber and tell him to go. His teammates perked their ears up and watched him closely as to be somewhat confused. We didn't really know what to do at that point and just looked at each other mysteriously and then Dad spoke again. "What are you all waiting for?" he asked. "Turn 'em loose but do it slowly." We proceeded to unyoke them two at a time and in a few minutes they were gone out of sight. This all seemed crazy to my brother and me but we had always had faith in our father and we intended for it to stay that way.

Thirty minutes went by and then an hour. Not a sound had been made and I began to doubt our day's efforts as a whole. All I could seem to think of was one giant question. How would we ever get them all back? As I said, I thought about it heavily but didn't make a sound verbally.

Suddenly, Dad spoke seriously again. "You guys are old enough now to learn another lesson and try to remember this one too. You'd think that a person could hear a dog bark anywhere on Cold Creek or Lenior Creek from here but that's all wrong. Come with me and let me prove another point to you boys."

Without a word, we followed him further on down the Old Bald Trail toward a specific point that I remember as one of the coldest places on earth called, "The Tree Stand." My brother and I had been to the Tree Stand with Dad many times but hadn't really paid a lot of attention as to notice the point he was getting ready to make.

The Tree Stand is nothing more than a small oak tree that is limbed to the ground making it easy to climb. It stands erect in a shaded north-side location in which the sun hardly ever warms. Galax is common there too and the ground looks like a giant green-colored bed comforter from its thickness.

After arriving there, Dad explained to us that the Dry Branch or the right fork of Cold Creek could only be heard from the Tree Stand location and made us promise not to forget it. We nodded our heads at him to assure our affirmation and all of us started listening for our thought-to-be lost hounds.

Then unexpectedly, we heard Timber begin to open up a good distance below us and the more he barked, more and more dogs joined in with him and in what seemed to be only seconds, we had a fine-sounding race on the way. The longer it went, the better it sounded and we started to get excited as usual.

The pack crossed the Old Bald Ridge into Lenior Creek trailing slowly. Dogs while running bear in this particular area of Cold Mountain will usually cross the Old Bald Trail through a Laurel cut just above a gap called The Stomp.

I'm not sure how The Stomp got its name but it is a beautiful open wooded saddle that is plentiful with Red Oak trees. It's about five hundred yards from the Tree Stand down the Old Bald Trail to the Stomp and the entire ridge is densely covered with Mountain Laurel and Ivy except for that picture-perfect gap.

The pack was presently in "bad country" as we called it because acres and acres of land there on the Lenior Creek side of Old Bald is rough going to say the least. Walking upright is almost an impossibility. Crawling is much faster and easier for most people and notice that my pen wrote most instead of all.

My grandpa Elb was an exception when it came to moving through thick Mountain Ivy bushes. Many of the elder men of our community have described to me numerous times about how Grandpa could walk up on top of them. I've tried it before and couldn't believe how difficult it was to keep my balance but it's been said that Mr. Elb was very talented at it.

All we could do was stay quiet and listen closely. We all hoped that they would move on through the most rugged part of the Old Bald Ridge before jumping their prey for if by chance they were to stop a bear there--getting to them with any success would be an almost automatic failure. The next few moments were critical and we stood silently paying close attention.

Just as I figured, the dogs suddenly jumped and headed for Fork Ridge of Lenior Creek. Dad and I started back up the Old Bald Trail after he instructed my brother to temporarily stay put at the Tree Stand. The pack sounded good as we climbed upon the high rocks of Old Bald again and our excitement levels were high. The pack didn't lack very far before topping Fork Ridge of Lenior Creek when they did an about face and began to go back the way they had come.

I had laid my rifle down to take the load off of my shoulders when we stopped on the Old Bald Rocks for the second time. When the dogs unexpectedly turned, I grabbed it quickly and as I put its leather strap over my head, my father asked me where I was going. I answered him with my intention of going back down the trail toward my big brother and he proceeded to talk me out of it. "Don't make any unnecessary noise," he said, so we sat quietly again and waited.

We knew Mark was paying very close attention at that point for he was then the one closest to the fine-sounding race. They sounded to cross a little lower toward the Stomp that time as they crossed the Old Bald Trail and my father and I made tracks for the Tree Stand one more time to rejoin my brother.

It only takes about eight to ten minutes to reach the Tree Stand from the Old Bald Rocks and it can be made a touch faster depending on how hot the pursuit is. We made the small trip quickly and just in time to hear the pack go out of hearing from Big Anderson Creek into the Right Prong of Cold Creek. Big Anderson Creek is quite a place in itself. The uppermost portion of it divides Lenior Creek and Cold Creek while the lower portion stands as the divider between Henderson Creek and Little Anderson Creek. Big Anderson is not near as vast as maybe Lenior Creek or Cold Creek but what real estate is consumed in it is that of rocky rough terrain. The woods in Big Anderson are some of the most beautiful in the Western North Carolina Mountains but most of it is on a significantly steep grade.

To our surprise, we found my brother amiss when we reached the Tree Stand. His tracks left behind in the damp leaves let us know that he had felt led to top the next ridge over to try to stay in hearing of the faster moving dogs. I was somewhat confused then but looked toward my dad for our next move. I was confident in his decisions concerning any matter and felt sure that he would lead us in the right direction whether it be good or bad.

He stared back at me with a defiant sort of look and said, "Let's go back son." By that time I had begun to memorize each little curve in the Old Bald Trail and even the fallen leaf patterns under my feet were starting to look familiar. In a few minutes we topped the Old Bald Rocks again and sat down to listen for the pack.

Dad then explained something to me that has been an asset to my hunting down through the years and I expect to never forget it. With his tone of voice down to a whisper, he proceeded to tell me that when dogs go out of hearing into Cold Creek from Anderson Creek a hunter after climbing up on the Old Bald Rocks could set his watch and wait. "In no more than fifteen minutes," he said, "the dogs will have had ample time to cross over the Old Bald Butt and pop back into hearing in the heart of Cold Creek. If their barks can't be heard by then, we'll go back to the Tree Stand and I will show you where to find them."

We sat quietly and the fifteen minutes seemed to be hours. As we waited, I started daydreaming as usual and for some reason thought of my grandpa Elb. I couldn't help but wonder how many times he had been where my dad and I were. I imagined him standing on the Old Bald Rocks wearing his brown Duck-back clothing that Grandma Sally had patched perfectly with his head to one side as to point his dominant ear down the main lead of Cold Creek. I was in another world when Dad bumped me to let me know that the time was up.

We didn't get in any rush down the trail for the third time and when we returned to the Tree Stand, we stopped for a thought to radio my brother and received no answer. I thought about where he could possibly be and knew that he had a workable walkie-talkie for I had loaned him mine that day being that his was on the blink. I laughed to myself as I thought back on the early morning hours when my brother borrowed the radio from me.

I've always been particular with my belongings whether it be clothing, boots, vehicles, tractors, dog leads, radios, guns and such and have made it a habit to take good care of my personal property in any situation. My brother being somewhat opposite and quite laid back had given me a serious look when I handed him my hand-held Midland and I tried to recollect if I had made any small gesture maybe to hurt his feelings. I couldn't remember, but I hoped I hadn't.

Seen here are my grandparents, Elbert and Sally Griffin, two people in which I often find myself thinking about. I miss them more and more with the passing of every day.

My brother and I had fought like cats and dogs in our younger years but when it came right down to it, we would have died for each other also. We always leaned on each other so to speak, one never letting the other down. Even though we looked quite different and had personalities that weren't the same, our brotherly love was that of unchanging. I thank God for that blessing and I'm proud of the fact that we still stand by each other today.

Standing at the Tree Stand for the third time, Dad and I couldn't hear even a faint noise of any kind that sounded like a dog barking. The pack had left Big Anderson Creek into the right prong of Cold Creek and entered a thicket that's incomparable to any on Cold Mountain.

Old Bald Butt divides the Left Prong and Right Prong of Cold Creek and approximately three hundred yards down it from the Old Bald Rocks, turns almost straight off making its name fit perfectly. Old Bald Butt is also very cliffy and when dogs cross over the butt, they can only be heard by those below them. Men while on top of Old Bald Butt has to rely solely on time when that happens and my father had taught me that lesson within the last hour.

Dad said nothing more and left the Tree stand on a slight downhill grade through the open woods of Big Anderson Creek toward the right prong of Cold Creek. In about ten minutes we came to a small gap on the next ridge over which divides the two larger creeks. This ridge intersects with the Old Bald Ridge and is known to us as the Shirt Sleeves.

It could easily be guessed why that woolly ridge is called the Shirt Sleeves, and believe me, it lives up to its name. I had been there before but had never fully understood its layout until my father taught me ever more that day. He explained to me of how listening closely from the Shirt

Sleeve Gap was very important in the process of finding dogs that suddenly seemed to have disappeared. Luckily, we didn't need to make our way down the thick Shirt Sleeve Ridge on that particular day but more about it could be written with adjectives of plenty.

My father proved himself to be correct for when we stepped to the edge of the pretty little gap we heard the faint echoes of the pack across one ridge deeper on the Right Prong of Cold Creek. I wasn't sure where they were but Dad whispered softly as to explain, "They're in the Dry Branch just as I figured," he said. He then proceeded to ask if I had learned something from that race and without saying a word, I answered him with my happy face.

"Your brother's a good way ahead of us," he said, "so we might as well take it easy." After further discussion, he had it figured that my brother Mark would bust a cap about the time we topped the next small ridge as to look straight down on him. We then decided that the muffled pack hadn't moved any in the last five minutes or so and agreed they were definitely treed.

As we walked and crawled toward the next finger-like ridge, I couldn't believe that the young pack had found their own track and had trailed together flawlessly to jump a bear. My dad and I quietly discussed their fine ability while on our way and he was as proud of them as I was.

I had pulled a thin jacket out of my vest during the fifteen-minute wait on Old Bald and gladly put it on. It's usually windy there and at an elevation of fifty-eight hundred feet the wind chill factor can lower body temperatures in a hurry. I didn't take time to pull it off before leaving the Tree Stand and had to stop briefly to do so just before topping our last and final ridge.

We could hear the pack well from there and Dad pointed toward them with a big grin on his face. I buttoned the big pocket on the back of my hunting vest quickly and was back on my feet in a flash. I leaned my head up over his shoulder to hear the instructions of his projected path through the rocky cove that lay before us. About that time, a blast echoed below us and I was glad to the bone because my big brother certainly deserved a moment of truth and I was proud for him.

I yelled a little with Dad looking strangely at me and we then proceeded down the steep mountainside in the direction in which the sound was coming from. We had to guess where the dogs were then for everything had suddenly gotten quiet. The excited little trek took us about twenty minutes but I finally spotted the white color on some of the dogs in the open valley below us.

My father and I joined the pack with some kind of great pride and petted each one with vigorous strokes from their ears to their tails. They seemed to know how proud we were of them and started barking again. It was a good feeling especially when I thought back of how sorry they used to be.

The bear was beautiful. Its coat was a shiny black. We figured it to weigh about two hundred and fifty pounds. I could foresee a hard time ahead in getting the animal out of the woods. Three men were sure to have an enormous job ahead for the rest of the day. At that point though, getting all of the dogs and the bear out of the woods was the least of our worries. When our excitement levels calmed a bit, we noticed that Mark was no where to be found.

The dogs were tied with pieces of nylon string. We knew he had been there with them but seemed to have mysteriously disappeared. We started yelling but heard no

answer. Something was wrong and we couldn't figure it out.
Dad tried to make me feel better and assured me that my
brother would be back in a few minutes, but deep inside, I
knew something was not adding up right.

I yelled again. That time to the top of my lungs. I
heard a faint hoot from the mountainside above me that
sounded to be at least two hundred yards away. I looked at
Dad and asked him his opinion of what was going on. He
shrugged his shoulders and then told me to go up the rough
cove and see while he stayed with the pack.

The whole time that I was climbing the steep ground
on my tired, rubbery legs, I was hoping and praying that my
big brother wasn't hurt.   That was the only logical
explanation I could think of and the further I went, the more
scared I became.

The hoots sounded closer and closer and I was afraid
of what I was going to find. I was suddenly out of open
woods and into thick Ivy bushes and I climbed with a rush.
My body was so exhausted that only the adrenaline kept me
putting my feet down at an even pace I reckon.

I came face to face with a huge rock in the thicket as
big as an average automobile and had to stop there
momentarily to breathe. I might have taken a thirty second
break and ripped around the big rock with a zip and was
startled by the happy face of my brother as he slid down the
mountain on the slick Red Oak leaves.

I couldn't believe it was him and was beside myself
to find out that he was alright. At first I spoke harshly as to
ask him what he was doing at least two hundred yards up the
mountainside from the treed pack and as he started to laugh I
got even madder. He couldn't seem to stop laughing and

being very perturbed, I asked him again concerning what the meaning of all this was.

"Do you think that I would have had the heart to tell you I'd lost your radio?" I couldn't believe it and asked if he had found it. "Yes," he said, "as a matter of fact I just had found it before you came around that huge rock." He proceeded to tell me the story of the bad feeling that appeared in his stomach after he got the bear down.

"I was so happy," he said, "and then I reached hurriedly into my vest pocket and suddenly found that your radio was missing. I knew that you would have a cow, so I then tied all of the dogs with string and started back tracking hoping to find it and I'm sure glad that I did."

I got tickled then and we both sat on the damp ground and had a hoot together. After we finally settled down I gladly took my radio back from him and turned it on to see if it would still work properly. The first transmission I made Chick answered and sounded as if he was beside himself. He was glad to hear the story and being that Glenn Browning was with him, we were relieved by his assuring us that Glenn would be on the way immediately to help us out.

Chick and Glenn Browning had been together fellow-shipping with a good friend of the party named Lester Heatherly who lived then and still does in the last house on Cold Creek in the Cruso Community.

Lester and his wife are some of the best people this world has ever known especially to a bunch of country boys such as my brother and me. Lester always asks as quick as he sees one of us how our family is doing. Him and his wife are very considerate of others and both of them are just plain out good folk.

Lester stands out in my mind as one of the best apple farmers that I've ever known. Lester and his wife kept their orchard tidy and ship shape for many years and I always looked forward to eating a fresh one right off of the tree on a cool fall day. I never asked him for one either because I knew I was more than welcome to help myself.

Lester and his wife still reside on Cold Creek in the same modest home but did finally retire from the apple orchard a few years back. Their memory will be with me as long as I live and I hope I can stand in Lester's yard for many more years to come enjoying a neighborly time together.

Mark and I rejoined Dad in a short while and after a bite of lunch, started our way down the right prong of Cold Creek slowly. Three men leading ten dogs and dragging a two hundred and fifty pound bear makes for a long evening and we welcomed the sight of Glenn as we approached the halfway point of the big cove.

The rest of our trip was hard to say the least but we kept working at it and finally the pasture field that belonged to Lester was in sight. Lester and Chick admired the brute and congratulated the dogs on a successful day in the woods.

I'd never seen my dad show his fatigue before but I noticed that day that he had been through enough. I was proud of my father though and felt good in knowing that he still lacked several hours being as tired as I was but I wouldn't have admitted it. Lester's dear wife asked my dad how in the world the four of us had made it out of the rough creek to civilization with the load we had. The answer he gave her that late evening described the situation perfectly. "It's a mystery to me ma'am," he said.

Pictured here are Mr. and Mrs. Lester Heatherly.
Words cannot start to explain the gratitude that my family has for
these two individuals. Mr. and Mrs. Heatherly are perfect
examples for young people to look at closely.

HIT OR MISS

The church bell rang with crystal clear sounds as to let the Dix Creek community know that Sunday School would start in five minutes. I had walked the brisk three-fourths of a mile to maybe work the soreness from my legs in which I hadn't mentioned to any of my family members. Truth is they probably had sore places too after the exhausting Saturday that we had experienced in the woods.

I was glad that Sunday was upon us because we desperately needed rest. I remember laughing out loud when I started to church at the seemingly nonexistent pack of hounds. I spoke to them as I passed by and each of them gave me a friendly look, but none of them seemed eager enough to greet me at the end of their chains. The Cold Mountain hunting trip that we were engaged in the day before had put a damper on their anxiety blasts and they rested quietly in the wooden doghouses bedded with straw.

The last week of the regular bear-hunting season had quickly approached us and I wondered how the time had slipped by so fast. I couldn't help but think of how time seemed to pass so slowly through the summer months, compared to its quick in and out modes during the hunting season. I enjoyed farming but a nice autumn day in the woods would overwhelm my wishes if a choice could possibly have been an option.

I felt good as I walked through the Church parking lot toward my parent's automobile after the morning service but not good enough to walk my way home as I had done earlier. It was uphill all the way back and since Sundays had a way of making me lazy anyway, I decided to ride.

By the time my Sunday clothes were hung on metal hangers in the third story closet of our log home, Mom had dinner on the table. A lot of folk call the evening meal "dinner," but at our house, it was known as "lunch". The evening meal was known to us as "supper". My mom didn't consider that to be bad manners and believe me, she knew the difference between good manners and bad.

As parents, I suppose a great percentage of us are guilty of not teaching our kids proper manners. I can honestly say that manners in my modern-day home falls significantly short of the standards that were set by my parents when I lived under their roof.

As youngsters, my brother and I answered our parents with a "sir" or a "ma'am". We also asked to be excused from the table after a meal. We were taught to speak to our elders with respect and by all means we were taught to treat people not only equally, but as if we would have wanted to be treated ourselves.

When their rules were broken, we paid the price and discipline in those days was quite a bit different than that of today. When we needed correcting, our parents used a belt or a keen switch and it was amazing how fast we would jump back into the routes of the long and narrow road, versus staying between the ditches of the wide and grassy one.

In those days, there was no counting "one," "two," and then you were in trouble on "three". We got what we deserved and were never struck by a lick that wasn't needed. I absolutely disagree with any sort of child abuse, but I can't help but believe that our society of the late 90's would be far better off if our discipline methods were somewhat recalled in our efforts of raising offspring. By doing so, us parents just might see today's younger generation become more responsible and trustworthy.

Monday morning had crept upon us and we suddenly realized that we had entered the last week of bear-hunting season. As I've stated earlier, that was somewhat of a scary thought because other than another short season toward the last of December, the hunting was over until the next fall. Ten months of keeping the pack chained seems to be much like a prison term for a hunter because the dogs require quality care every day of the year.

Caring for a pack of hounds through the winter, spring, and summer months is much of a challenge. Most people probably don't realize the attention that must be appropriated to good dog care. Their feeding habits must change in the off season to keep them somewhat physically fit along with seeing that their living quarters are clean.

Old bedding must be disposed of in the warmer months to control flea problems, accompanied with proper chemical treatments as necessary. Keeping all of the chains and running cables properly maintained is quite a job in itself also. Hunting dogs require daily attention three hundred and sixty-five days a year and that's a considerable price to pay for the privilege of hunting them for only an average of six weeks.

We loaded our pack that Monday morning and struck out to start the last week with what we thought would be a bang. We were off to Bear Pen Ridge on Dix Creek since we hadn't disturbed it at all on Saturday. The long rough two track road to Bear Pen Ridge made my dad's truck rock back and forth. For that reason, staying awake was difficult along with the warm air from the heater blowing at my feet. I just wasn't up to it that particular morning but when the gear shift hit the park position, I made myself become a part of the rush.

We made our way as a group up the steep trail to the Bear Pen Rocks and arrived there just after daybreak. The view was not good that Monday morning for the fog was down, cutting visibility to near nothing. I shouldn't have, but I allowed the lousy feeling that I was experiencing to get the best of me after I observed how wet the bushes were from the fog in the early hour.

At that point, I would rather have turned back and called it a day but I didn't want to say anything to reveal that. My body ached and my head hurt but I kept trudging on. At one time, I felt so bad that I came close to handing the leash in which the two dogs I was leading were on to another of the party and head back to the truck. I hated for a single man to be bothered with four dogs though and continued the journey.

I felt a touch better when we finally turned downhill into the Bear Pen Gap. The fog was thick and our clothes were heavily dampened by it. We continued on even though we were quite miserable. Everyone seemed to be somewhat discouraged when my dad suddenly halted the party explaining quickly that he had found a track in which the strike dog could smell.

The young dog "Timber" was quite fooled by the age of the track that morning because after the turn loose, the pack cold trailed completely out of our hearing and still hadn't got their prey on its feet. That particular situation simply occurs sometimes when hunting with dogs and as it happened, we were on a goose chase for the remainder of the day.

That Monday made very little history to be remembered because we lost our pack and finally found them late in the evening strung out in the Shining Creek section of the Big East Fork of the Pigeon. One by one, at last we recovered all of them a good bit after dark and made our way home to do the farming chores by flashlight.

Monday of the last week had been a failure but we made the best of it and Mom's cooking tasted better than ever. We had decided before breaking up, to rest the pack on Tuesday morning but hunting plans were made for a big Wednesday adventure.

By bedtime it was snowing outside. The drastic change of weather was sort of unusual for that early autumn part of the year and it seemed to add a new glimmer of excitement into the air at our home. As a young lad, I couldn't wait for the snow to fall each year. It's hard to explain why some folk's opinions change as they become older but fifteen years later finds me not looking forward to winter time at all, much less the snow.

The forecast was predicting only a couple of inches for the lower elevations of the Western North Carolina mountains, but a much more significant accumulation for the higher ones. The part of the forecast that sounded most intriguing to us was when the Meteorologist predicted the small front to move through our area rather quickly. He figured the precipitation to be ending just after midnight, leaving our Wednesday hunt right on schedule.

Four a.m. struck chimes on Mom's grandfather clock that sat lifelike in her orderly living room and my brother and I rushed to the door to observe the overnight accumulation. To our surprise, the ground was barely covered with the white stuff. We had a name for a small dusting such as we had received. It was known to us as a "skift". I remember my father saying many times, "No big deal boys, it is just a little skift."

We allowed a few extra minutes that morning before going outside to grease our leather boots to the hilt. We enjoyed hunting in snow but it can quickly cause a miserable day in the woods if feet become wet too early. Our boots had been greased the night before, but Dad allowed that another fast shot couldn't hurt them. Even though the leather had probably soaked up all the grease it could hold, "An extra coat on the outside could only help", he said.

The young pack was eager to go that early day and loaded with no problems. It seemed strange to button the side vents in the closed position on the plywood dog box to cut the cold airflow off of the dogs while traveling on the highway. The first frozen precipitation of the year has always been hard for me to believe along with the cold air that accompanies it.

We reached Frank's store to find "Chick" in good spirits and seemed to be over ripe to hear another race. He smiled from ear to ear just talking about the possibility of finding a hot track. Henry was proud of the young pack and bragged openly on them in the store. He seemed proud also to be a part of the clan and wanted everyone to know it.

The clan had cast their votes the night before for a next day rendezvous to Crawford's Creek located at the upper most portion of the Cruso community. A somewhat significant report has been documented in a previous chapter concerning the geographical layout of Crawford's Creek but enough could never be said as to describe the beautiful and majestic scenery there.

I'm surely guilty of taking for granted on numerous occasions the beauty of a particular spot in Crawford's Creek that is located where the Crawford's Creek and John's Cove Creeks intersect. That unique creek-side setting includes an age-old house known to most natives as the Harrison Reece house.

A small dusting of snow, known to country folk as a "skift."

Seen here is a portion of the Crawford's Creek Road that winds beside the fluent waters of Crawford's Creek.

I'm privileged to be from a family in which relatives of mine owned the house at one time. Harrison Reece was the father of Mrs. Willie Mae Griffin who is the wife of my dad's brother, Hershel. Mr. Reece sold the house in 1950 and moved to Washington State for whatever reasons unknown.

Nevertheless, I feel as if I've been on a trip in an inescapable story book of fine fantasies every time I pass by the old house and view the aged fruit trees and the different garden spots there. I've also tried to imagine the number of kids that have been raised there through the years and envied their freedom from the noisy stress-filled days in which we now live.

I've caught myself daydreaming many times about my Aunt Willie Mae playing in the near by creeks during a hot summer month of long ago when she was a child. She's discussed with me before, of the team of steers that Mr. Reece kept there to tend crops and to drag logs with also.

Their names were Bob and Wiley. From what I can gather, these steers were of the truest quality. Their head sense was top of the line also. I'm not certain of their particular breed, but more than one old timer has described them to me as having horns and their color was that of dark red. Work steers such as Bob and Wiley are few and far between these days but still make fond memories fonder to many folk in this country I'm sure especially the older ones.

We walked quietly as a group that morning by the forks of the two creeks making our way up the Crawford's Creek side and entered into a place called the Pete Field. The Pete Field is located on a south-side slope and is the last open space on what some would call the Deep Gap Road before entering into continuous acres of timber.

This photograph is of the Harrison Reece house in Crawford's Creek. Even at its old age it still stands proudly erect.

Seen here is my respected Uncle Hershel and Aunt Willie Mae.

The Pete Field was crop tended for many years prior to mid century and as we made our way through it I thought of Bob and Wiley. As I kept a steady pace, I wondered how many hard days the two work steers had endured there. I imagined them on brisk frosted white mornings just like the one I was experiencing pulling logs off of the Pete Fields' gentle slopes as to make their way toward the big Reece house heavily loaded.

At the upper end of the Pete Field, my wondering thoughts of the old days left just as they had come and hunting bear was back to foremost in my mind again. As our party entered the woods out of the Pete Field, the bare dawn of light got dark again caused from the treetops over our heads. I remember being somewhat humored by watching my fellow hunters feeling of their garments trying to remember which pocket they had stored their hand-held flashlights in just minutes before as we all stumbled along.

Just above the Pete Field, the most used and main logging road in which we were traveling starts forking and the small tributary roads off of it are several in count. Trying to explain the layout of each of them with a pencil would be a near about impossibility, but my dad had his mind set to take our hounds out a particular one called the Chick Stand Road.

The name of that road could be somewhat misleading to a reader but, yes, Henry was the reason for its so-called name. I'm not sure of all of the exacts of his previous incidents there, but Chick had fired a few caps from the old logging path in the days when he was physically able.

The Chick Stand Road is level for the most part and is extremely enjoyable to walk with leashed dogs. It's steep upper-side banks show thorough tracks of wildlife crossings and seeing a plain bear track in fresh black dirt had a way of adding excitement to a cool morning hunt beyond degree. Most hunters will declare good faith in their strike dog's word but seeing toe prints in the dirt back that opinion up immensely.

Pictured here is what remains of the small clearing known to our party as the Pete Field. It was an open pasture when I was young but has grown over slowly as time has passed.

The Chick Stand Road winds in and out of several coves and we had made our way that morning to a small creek known as Pine Stand Branch. It's been called that as long as I can remember and as we were making our way across the small brook, I looked ahead just in time to see my distant father giving a hand signal for the pack to halt immediately. At that moment, I knew we were on to something that was good for excitement and suddenly felt good about the situation. We were definitely in the heart of bear country and stood there briefly on nervous, anxious feet.

The only worry for me was knowing that Sailor wasn't along. Even though I had quite a sound faith in the young dog "Timber," my stomach couldn't help but to have a weary, worry-some feeling. I remember discussing the matter momentarily with my brother and eventually just stopped talking because it was evident that each of us were only trying to make the other feel better.

After what seemed to be an eternity, Dad was in view again and motioned for us to bring the pack on toward him. Approaching him at a close distance, I noticed a big grin on his face and instantly felt better about our early morning adventure. A smile such as that had to be carrying a bag full of confidence with it.

We took a few seconds to chitchat with him. He explained how the young dog had performed well in tracking the bear through its feeding ground and on toward water. Very hurriedly, he also let us know that he and Timber had tracked the bruin from where it had drank to just beyond the next small ridge top and was confident that it was laying in a dense Laurel thicket on the next cove to our right called Basin Branch.

Basin Branch on Crawford's Creek has probably been seen the least by humanity than any other cove there. Basin

Branch is where the Chick Stand Road comes to an end. It's a secret way to the high top of Cold Mountain and is by far the closest way also compared to a long trip of back tracking the Chick Stand Road to the Deep Gap Trail.

Basin Branch is heavily congested with Mountain Laurel and Ivy for a short distance from the end of the Chick Stand Road but ceases quickly. Basin Branch then turns to a grassy oak filled cove but remains very steep as it ascends toward the main ledge of Cold Mountain.

With confusion at a surprising minimum the hounds were loosed in a single file manner and we had another fine sounding race in the makings within a matter of seconds. The pack went left out of Basin Branch back toward Pine Stand and in minutes had fastly faded out of our hearing toward the main body of Crawford's Creek. Their quality sound had sprayed a fog of excitement into the air that was making hot feet for all of us.

My brother had chosen to follow the pack up the steep grade in which they had left so my dad and I back tracked the Chick Stand road as quickly as possible. I ran so hard that my side began to hurt. I guess most everybody has had that happen to them at one time or another. The jarring mode of a run causes the plague-like symptoms and even though it makes for quite a comical situation, its seriousness always overrides the laughs and changes them to frowns eventually.

Limping and somewhat dragging one leg, I was determined to stay in sight of my father who hadn't even thought about looking back. He had nothing on his mind but the location of the fast moving pack and seeing him stop momentarily to listen for them overjoyed me. He finally noticed my ailment and inquired quietly. "It's just my side," I said, "it'll be all right in a minute."

The dogs couldn't be heard from where we were standing and Dad decided to check with Chick to see if by chance he had heard them long enough to declare an accurate direction. Chick was out of his truck at the time straining his ears as to listen for a faded race and didn't answer until Dad had transmitted at least three or four times. "I do hear dogs", Henry said. "Go towards Frady's Orchard!" he exclaimed, "I'm thinking they are headed for Dog Loser Ridge."

Dad didn't take the time to answer him back. The small radio antenna closed into his walkie- talkie in a flash and we were on our way again at top speed bound for Frady's Orchard.

Frady's Orchard on Crawford's Creek is a very well-known place to most people of the Cruso Community especially hunters. The most used path from the Maple Ford to the U.S. Forest Service boundary forks just past the Old Reece house for the second time and staying left there leads directly into the aged apple orchard that was then owned by Mr. Hugh Frady. Mr. Frady's camp house still sits quietly by in the lower most corner of the orchard and is a most peaceful sight to see especially when the fall colors are climaxed.

Frady's Orchard wasn't an hour's journey for my dad and me to say the least, but was a considerable distance to travel from whence we came to find that Chick had given us unintentional false information. The dogs he had heard were not ours but belonged to the hunters of a small game caliber and my father and I were beside ourselves when we were made aware of the fact.

Needless to say, Chick was slightly reprimanded on the hand-held radio and together we started the ascension back toward the Chick Stand Road, grouching with every step of the way. I could tell that my father was on the verge of aggravation and I stayed silent just to make sure that no more fuel was added to the fire.

Thirty hard minutes and several drops of sweat later, we finally made it back to where we had turned the hounds loose. The woods around us were silent in all directions. Standing together very confused our next move was undetermined to say the least. Both of us sat down on an oak log that had fallen at its ripe age to recollect our thoughts and try to make some kind of reasonable sense out of all the last hour's chaos.

Having viewed our options carefully we decided to hike toward the end of the Chick Stand Road being as we had listened all of the coves to our left as we journeyed back. Even though Chick's inadequate directions had annoyed us slightly, we had no hard feelings. Incidents such as what had transpired that morning just go hand in hand with the sport of bear hunting and must be tolerated from time to time. Being aware of that fact, my father and I realized that confusion was a thorn in our side for the day and simply agreed to deal with it.

At that time, my dad and I started our walk again but slowed our pace substantially as we reentered the cove on the Chick Stand Road called Pine Stand. Feeling fairly fatigued we stooped low to the ground on our hands and knees to consume a fresh cold drink of water from the small brook. Seemingly from nowhere the pack suddenly entered Pine Stand Cove with a roar at a significantly higher altitude above us.

At that point we didn't really know what was going on but the spirit of excitement had unexpectedly stiffened the air again and like a dream come true, two down-and-out hunters were miraculously changed into lucky chaps that were overly ready to participate in some action. That's the part I like best about bear hunting in the Great Smokies. A person can be completely out of the picture during one minute and suddenly be caught in the center of the camera's eye the next.

The raging dogs came into the heart of Pine Stand Cove and gradually slowed to a stop. We were listening and started our ascension immediately. Pine Stand Cove off of the Chick Stand Road is that of rough terrain as most of the coves are but is quite a bit more than normal to be located on a south-side slope. Jagged rock of all sizes cover its floor from bottom to top making the hike up it quite treacherous at times.

About halfway up the steep cove, my father and I stopped for a short breather. The dogs were still ringing with yelps of encouragement but they seemed to be moving small distances periodically. That gave us the impression that the pack was just bayed in the thick Ivy. Being made aware of that, we gave ourselves only a slight glimmer of hope for success being that we were approaching them uphill instead of down.

It's a hunter's best bet when stalking prey that has been temporarily stopped by a pack of hounds to arrive in a downhill direction especially when black bears are involved. There's no factual evidence to prove this explanation but I have found it to be true on many occasions. When approaching a pack from below them, their prey will usually make a last-minute break to run or jump when human scent is detected at an unsafe distance. The phenomenon of scent is still a mysterious equation for me to produce an adequate formula for and will remain so indefinitely I'm sure.

A few moments later and several hundred feet higher in elevation, we found ourselves surrounded by the distinct sounds of the dogs and were certainly close enough to take things seriously. The trees seemed to rattle from their loud barks of eagerness and my mind entered that unique mode of super concentration.

The moment of truth had slipped upon us quickly. For no reason, the thought suddenly occurred to me as to question the whereabouts of my long-gone brother. I sensed he was close and wondered if our presence was in his favor or not. I nudged my dad below the thigh with the barrel of my Winchester to prompt his attention. He turned his head slowly my way and we had a whispering chat as to guess which direction my brother was entering from. It was a most strategic time.

At that particular moment I remember thinking about the fine times my God had allowed me to share with my dad and was somewhat astonished, as usual, to suddenly realize that he had permitted me to be standing in the midst of what I enjoyed the most from life--again. The thing that plants a man's feet firmly on the freshly fallen October leaves is knowing that just being there is strictly a blessing in itself.

Keeping up with whose club is winning or losing isn't worth anything. Unlike most sports, hunting shouldn't have a scorekeeper. Just knowing that each day on a bear hunt promises something different--something unrepeatable--something that is up and beyond unique--is more than enough to make me aware of the fact that I am an undisputable winner as the sun sets in its orange western seat at the close of every day.

Winning, in that way makes a man wealthy beyond all degrees. And even if the jingle in his pocket is so little that he can barely hear it, a man that has enjoyed a good day in the woods with his hounds holds the wealth of the world safely in his palm. Standing there among the roaring young pack accompanied by my dad that day, with my pants holey, and the sole loose on one of my boots, I suddenly understood all of these factors and felt rich from the heart and that's what counts in a man's short life.

A faint glimmer of dim sunlight peeped through the lap of a large Mountain Red Oak tree and we slipped a few feet closer to the action. Our simple technique of crawling the last few feet was up in the air for being successful because the snow under us was frozen about one inch thick. That made staying on our feet less noisy than manipulating on our hands and knees. We could hear popping sounds coming from the mouth of the prey but still more Ivy bushes were blocking our sight. Just before our next and last movement, an unexpected blast from above seemed to lift our bodies off of the ground.

In no time flat, the pack faded hurriedly up the steep incline toward the Cold Creek side of Cold Mountain and was out of our hearing in a matter of minutes. My brother spoke with a shaken excited voice to make a statement of an unconfident explanation that he wasn't sure what had happened concerning his last-second shot. It was quite evident that the bear wasn't wounded to any sort of harsh extent because it left our presence on an uphill grade, which proved the matter. My brother didn't speak again and was gone with no more discussion. At that point, I shifted myself into an overdrive gear. I quickly told my father that I would see him later and without anymore thought started parting the Ivy bush branches toward the Cold Mountain Top. One of the finer points of Cold Mountain laid ahead of me that day and is the part of the mountain that heads off Pine Stand Cove. That point is called Green Knob.

Green Knob earned its name honestly for it is thickly covered with a plush carpet of Mountain Ivy making foot travel near impossible. I've crawled many times through the dense thickets of Green Knob and it looked as if this day was going to be no exception. Sometimes, I think that the mysterious whereabouts of the long lost pack was all that kept one going that day.

I pushed and pushed through the heavily congested branches lunging with every fiber of my soul toward the top. The afternoon hours were upon me by that time and even though the temperature was somewhat comfortable in the valley from whence I had come, the higher elevated portion of Cold Mountain was down right frigid. It seemed to be getting colder by the minute especially with a considerable wind chill involved.

Snow was also beginning to play a role too in conquering the task of climbing Green Knob. It was approximately four to six inches deep there and the wind was howling. The snow was coming down in sheets much like a spring rain. The weather had suddenly taken a turn for the worse but trudging onward was an absolute.

I didn't have any idea where my brother was again. I guess it didn't really matter at that point, but I knew the disappeared pack needed to be located soon, for the day was long past half gone. The snow began to fall heavier and heavier and the temperature seemed to be dropping by the minute as I made my way closer to the top of Green Knob.

In spite of the terrible conditions, I pushed onward and finally made it into the Cold Mountain Top Trail if it can still be called one. The old foot trail is grown over with brush of all descriptions even until this day, which makes traveling it nearly as difficult as not having a trail at all. Climbing upon the rocks of Green Knob caught me totally by surprise. The ice was approximately one inch deep there making a haven for slippery steps.

Seen here in the distance, Green Knob sits among the high top of Cold Mountain. Its up-right posture heads off the gulching acres of land found in the upper-most portions of Cold Creek.

My face froze to a stiff clammy statue immediately when the frigid north wind that was blowing up Cold Creek hit me. Its severity was that of an arctic blast and my wet hair changed instantly from fine thin lines to hard, complex strands much like that of a steel brush. My mustache froze also making my upper lip extremely hard to maneuver and ice quickly built up around my nostrils. I listened down Cold Creek very hurriedly because surviving for any length of time on the rock would have been an absolute impossibility.

Luckily I did hear the dogs and their tree barks were unmistakable.

After crawling my way off of the slick rocks into the grown over trail, I made my way down the leading ridge line, watching for a distinct small cove to my left which I knew was open and virtually free from Ivy bushes. As soon as I discovered the small cove's unforgettable details, I was ever so glad to lose elevation down it toward the yelping stationary pack.

It was quite evident by their sounds that they, much like me, had seen the better part of the day. Their tree barks were of a much slower pace than normal and each bark seemed to end in a tired moaning noise. At that moment, it dawned on me that the young pack of hounds had proven themselves over the last four weeks. I suddenly felt pity for them and even though I was cold, hungry, and in somewhat of a suffering state myself, I put forth a last blast of energy as to make my way onward through the fresh snow that had so quickly fallen.

They were treed among a boundary of Hemlock trees in a particular place located in the upper most portion of Cold Creek called the Laying Rock. I'm not sure how that name came into being but I'm sure it had something to do with the large boulders that I was currently drudging over, under, and around.

When at last I approached the tall evergreens, I noticed the satin black dog slayer on a hefty limb just beyond the reach of the pack. My Winchester came level. I realized that all was well and enjoyed knowing that another special time in a hunter's life had come to pass. As I proceeded to pull steadily on the gun's trigger, I noticed another rifle out of the corner of my eye. If was aimed slightly upward and looking down it's barrel was my brother who I was so glad to see.

The powder blasts echoed together chalking up another checkered flag for the tired dogs who had done more than their fair share to complete a race that had consisted of many cautions. My brother and I shook each other's cold hand, which reminded us of our poor physical conditions. We were near the frostbite stage and were starting to deteriorate noticeably.

We didn't even bother with looking at the prey we had taken. Instead my eyes seemed to be pulled by the notice of small, dry, twiggy, branches extending themselves outward from the bottom of the mid-sized Hemlock trees. I glanced at my brother's cold face and his expression assured me that he was thinking the same thing I was.

Getting a fire started was top priority at that stage of the game so we proceeded to break small brush from the pines and frantically placed small pieces of paper towels from our pockets under them. In about five minutes our fire was going well enough to add bigger pieces of wood and in less than fifteen minutes, we were enjoying waist high flames. We stood close to start a major warm up procedure as soon as possible.

We sat quietly rubbing our hands together by the fire and I thought about what we had just experienced together. Especially the part where my brother and I didn't tie the dogs after the shooting had taken place. That's usually a must when a bear is taken but I guess the physical conditions that we had been misfortunate enough to experience had made us somewhat selfish or should I say concerned.

When we warmed our bodies back to a so-called normal temperature we then received our fair share of humor for the day as we watched our fine young pack, one by one, come to the fire to join us. In a matter of minutes all of them were sitting by the fire as if they were human too. My brother and I sat in tears from our laughter. We petted them with firm strokes on their cold heads and enjoyed some time just looking at them and thinking back of how hard work and long hours had paid off.

At that special point in our lives, my brother and I knew that we had succeeded in a task that few people ever get the enjoyment of trying. Our love for that pack was enormous and all of them seemed to understand how we felt about them. They were made, as Grandpa would have put it and our laughs suddenly turned into serious grateful looks. We had done our job right that 1983 fall season, but most of the credit was to be handed to the dogs for we then knew that they had given one hundred percent of themselves.

We finally came back to the present situation at hand and figured we should try a hand-held radio transmission hoping that someone would answer. The first try we made, our father came back to us and was glad to hear the good news. He let us know that he had several guys to come in with him to help and assured us that he knew where we were and would be there shortly.

He advised us to stay by the fire until they arrived and just before signing our conversation off he asked a simple question figuring I guess to get a simple answer, "Who got the bear?" Not knowing what had really transpired hours before when the bruin had unexpectedly made a break by my brother, I looked over at him with a sneaky, mischievous grin and transmitted back slowly, "Let's just say, hit or miss we finally got the job done."

UNFORGETABLE

In late evening, the day after my near frostbite incident, I took a stroll to a one-acre back field which lays point blank beside the smooth running East Fork of the Pigeon River. In that field, I had planted a measured portion of annual Rye grass seed for a winter cover crop three weeks prior and had decided on the spur of a moment to go check its germination percentage or "how good of a stand I had," as my grandpa would have phrased it.

Visiting his family who resides close by this small plot of farming land was an adequate friendly being by the name of Don Rogers. Don has certainly been a perfect example for us young boys to follow all through our growing-up years. I spotted him standing by the warped old woodworking shop of the late Mr. Claude Deaver who was his father in law and he seemed to be admiring the plush green carpet of freshly sown grass. His hand went up of course to say "hello" as soon as he noticed me glimpse his way.

Don had some experience with hunting in his lifetime and he always seems to enjoy the excitement of a heated bear tale. There are many people that I know who don't have a lot of use for a gun but enjoy hearing stories of someone else becoming the main attraction of a tight squeeze in the woods.

Don has had much practice at hearing every kind of story known to man because of the career he has chosen to make his living at. He has been a barber of our community for as long as I can remember and I guess he's heard as much barber-shop gossip as any man on this earth--some true and some not. Don's the type of fellow who could easily tell the difference but would never make a peep as to disagree.

Everyone likes Don and he's lived his life in such a way as to not change that.

A Rye grass cover crop as seen in the photo, adds a much needed tint of green to the dull months of winter.

He listened very intently as I descriptively unfolded the saga of the day before. He shrugged his shoulders insinuating a shiver when I came across the part about nearly freezing to death and periodically glanced over his shoulder toward Cold Mountain as the story unfolded.

Our visitation was somewhat of a blessing that evening. Having neighbors such as Don made me realize how lucky I was to have dependable friends scattered throughout our cozy little community. Good friends and good fellowship among them are the foremost factors that inspired me to write this chapter.

Don Rogers, the community barber,
a friend to all.

As I walked through the crisp grass toward my truck, I thought about friendships in general and felt good inside about the close-knitted relationship of our hunting party. I also thought about the importance of those close friendships as the Creator above carefully inserts them into a person's vaporous life. It simply takes my breath away at times to recall numerous good days with my friends.

I traveled up the Dix Creek road very slowly and it suddenly dawned on me that we were down to the last hunt of the 1983 regular bear season. Saturday evening at sundown would mark its close and it finally became reality to me as I parked my truck on the long cement drive of home.

Thinking back on it, I remember debating with myself the possibility of ending the season with somewhat of a bang. The fine year had been good to us already, but I figured that one more well-spent day in the woods couldn't hurt anything. It seemed that every time I experienced a most cherished, memorable-hunting trip I was constantly looking forward to the next one.

Friday night had crept up on us quickly and the last day was suddenly near. Not cool, but down right cold temperatures had blasted into the Western North Carolina area with what seemed to be the most powerful front of the season. The twenty degrees felt like zero when the evening hours of dusk fell. It looked as if winter had blown our way at least for a time even though autumn still existed on the calendar for quite a while.

Chick had visited our home that brisk Friday night and sat with us by the rock fireplace enjoying the warm waves of hickory wood heat that so gracefully transformed from it. I remember us hulling and eating fresh chestnuts that had been roasted to near perfection in a black, worn baking pan that lay close to the coals on the smoothly cemented hearth. Our natural snack was accompanied with fresh, hot coffee and we reminisced together over past experiences of all kinds from work to play. I felt good when Chick was present and always looked forward to him coming to our house.

About 8:00 p.m., my father made his way to the thick Hemlock door of the big log house to take a peek outside and check the current thermometer readings. Turning back relatively fast he shrugged his neck down into his shoulders and made a whistling, blowing sound, which let us know that the temperatures had only gotten lower.

He said, "Chick, she'll be rough on a body in the morning." Henry answered boldly letting my dad know that there was no backing out of the last day's hunt. "You boys are tough--I've got faith in you," he said. He proceeded to say, "It'll get better after sunrise with a sneaky conspicuous grin on his face. Henry then got up slowly and made his way toward the door slinging his Big Ben jumper over his back. "See you fellows in the morning," he said, and was gone.

The big door was shut and locked for the night and final preparations were made for the bedtime hours. I used to thoroughly enjoy watching my dad bank the fireplace with wood for the night. He had a special way of filling the large firebox full of wood without smothering it. I guess that skill came about from much practice but nevertheless he was especially good at it.

The warmly quilted bed felt good but lasted for what seemed only minutes. I went out like a light and the next thing I heard was that distinct sounds of iron skillets touching together as my mom started the breakfast pro-cedure. That noise had a unique way of encouraging us to get out of bed for her morning meals could make a person walk through fire to them.

174

Pictured here is the rock fireplace in the log home of which I was raised. The many nights that my family and I spent by it will remain precious in my memory forever.

"Better dress warm", my dad said to my brother and me. "It's sure enough cold," he profoundly stated, "but the sky's clear making it a perfect day for hunting." My brother and I always heeded what our father told us and dressed with an extra layer in front of the fireplace. I can still hear my dad explaining on many occasions that clothes were easily taken off, but hard to put on when they didn't exist.

Mom followed us to the door as she always did cramming last-minute snack items into our hunting vest pockets. She had everything from apples to nuts and candy waiting close by for early-morning stuffers. She was never satisfied either until a sufficient amount of each was securely tucked away.

My big brother and I didn't quite appreciate her efforts as maybe we should have. She looked after us in every possible way and now that both of us are parents ourselves, we can scan back with some sorts of shame, realizing her genuine motherly love and care for us.

I often dwell on thoughts of my mother, especially during my childhood years. I distinctly remember the sick times that I experienced as a young lad. She would never leave my side for hours at a time. Life wasn't exactly easy for a young mother back then. That was over thirty years ago and I can recall her performing the everyday household duties without modern-day appliances which make them much less complicated now.

While electric washing machines were quite a popular item in just about every household, clothes dryers were few and far between. An automatic dishwasher was scarcely heard of and a microwave oven was some sort of a distant year two thousand machine only read about in books of the far-off future. An upright vacuum was only seen once in a great while and to say the least, throw away diapers were only good for a laugh.

Recollecting past memories such as these should make all of us feel different about our mother's funny little ways. Putting ourselves in their distant shoes if only for a minute, we would easily have a different perspective concerning parenthood.

We stepped out into the fresh morning air not knowing what the day held in store for us. It's probably a good thing we didn't because the happenings that lay ahead were somewhat extravagant, some for good and some for bad. Looking back on it all is quite a chore for me even until this day.

The pack had rested sufficiently and seemed ready for the next page to turn. Even Sailor was out that early morning with barks of eagerness and I was amused by the words Dad so seriously spoke to him as he unsnapped the chain from his collar. "I was gonna leave you here old man, but its the last day of the season--let's give it one more shot," he said. Sailor followed him to the truck with rich gleaming sparkles in his eyes. We all suddenly became silent while Sailor loaded himself. Our respect for him was that of an unknown caliber and while my brother and I would have rather left the former boss at home to enjoy his retirement, we respected our father's decision even though we were positive of it being Sailor's last trip to the woods for sure.

There's a lot to be learned from old animals I suppose. Their integrity never seems to die although their last days are upon them. They keep striving for another chance to do what they do best. Sailor had to know that it was virtually over for him but he still found energy from within and was determined to try one more time, if only for a few hours.

The tailgate was shut some few minutes later and we were off. A good friend came down the road about that time who I'm privileged to be related to as a first cousin. He's a Griffin too with first and middle names of George Sheridan. He's a happy go-lucky chap who's always looking for a good experience with the hounds.

My cousin Sheridan comes from a family that were top of the line. His father was the oldest of the eight children belonging to my grandparents, Elb and Sally Griffin. His name was Glenn. He has been mentioned in a previous chapter along with my deepest respects for him.

Sheridan is a lot like my Uncle Glenn in many ways. He not only looks like him but his actions favor his dad's in many ways. Much like his father, Sheridan loves kids of all ages and the kids seem to be attracted to him too, much like I was with his dad when I was a young lad. Sheridan's always good for a laugh also which brings us to the next part of the plot that cold morning.

As his truck came to a stop parallel to ours the conversation began. He shined a flashlight through the window and as its rays landed harshly on my brother and me and with a smile on his face, he asked. "How many clothes can you boys wear at one time? It's only twenty degrees this morning not ten," he stated. We didn't mind his nagging for we knew he was only kidding and besides, that was normal for him.

We enjoyed our cousin Sheridan when we were younger especially when it came to going places. He was young at heart back then and even in the present, he can still physically do most whatever he wishes to. Good health is something we should be thankful for on a regular basis and he's living proof of that.

His laughing about our excessive layers of clothing finally died out so to speak and our minds were then engaged into much more serious thoughts such as where we were going hunting which hadn't been fully settled the evening before. My father nodded at Sheridan from the shadowed truck cab and said, "Let's think about it for a few more minutes or at least until we get to the store."

The old truck was cold inside as it rolled stiffly down the two-track road. Its heater hadn't had enough time to be warm and our breath began to fog the windshield. Slightly cracking the windows to resolve the problem was a near necessity but the cold air that whistled through them was a touch more than fresh. It was down right cold but we didn't really pay it any attention because our thoughts were on to the hunt.

George S. Griffin, a person who always makes time for the kids.

A second cup of coffee hit the spot as our hunting group congregated in Frank's warm country store. Several jokes had to be snickered at concerning the amount of clothes that my brother and I were wearing due to cousin Sheridan's sneaky way of telling the entire party. We just grinned about it though and were glad that everybody had enjoyed some good early morning humor. We left Frank's on a high note and headed toward the West Fork of the Pigeon River, which had been decided on with a last-minute decision to end the first and regular season on Fork Mountain.

Big Rock House Cove was the selected run of the day and as we leashed the pack in pairs, Chick did what he could to lend a helping hand while rifles and vests were put in place on our backs. He wished us luck along with his usual last minute advice, one of which I wished later that I had listened more closely to concerning crossing the icy river.

The Big Rock House Trail consists of approximately one hundred and fifty yards in length from its take off to the river's edge. It declines elevation quickly in that so called stretch also making it quite a bit easier going but much more difficult coming back. The old path fades away within one hundred feet of the water due to years gone by with no trimming. That part of the trail is heavily congested with Mountain Laurel making dog leading much of a chore.

Bursting out of the dense Laurel onto the rocky bank of the rushing river, we suddenly noticed the first significant obstacle of the day. My cousin Sheridan slipped on the rocks that unexpectedly seemed to be greased. He wasted no time in letting the entire group know that the round river rocks were coated with a thin layer of clear ice. We hadn't noticed the dilemma we were up against but when we did, the thoughts of crossing the raging water put each of us into a most serious state of mind.

Under normal, ideal conditions, crossing the river without getting at least one foot wet was less than average. The cold temperatures had left the silent ice on the rocks and it covered them all over like it had been sprayed on with some sort of machine. Fording the river across them was to be a most difficult task, especially with a dog leash in one hand or the other.

There was no room for a mistake but as luck ran short on my behalf, I experienced a shocking crunch in the next few seconds that would prove to be a learning mishap. I was too eager to start the day of hunting I suppose. No matter how anxious a body is at any given moment, he or she should always remember that safety must be top priority and it would have been great that morning if my priorities had been in order.

Jumping the ice-covered rocks without falling had entered my mind but taking enough time to carefully do so proved to be my costly error. At midstream I slipped with one foot and after much effort to recover, finally went into the ice-cold river onto my side. The frigid liquid wrapped excitedly over my chest cavity and made its way up to my shirt collars.

My breath was that of little at that point. The cold shock was close to unbearable. As could easily be imagined, I got my feet back under myself in a matter of seconds and proceeded to the rocky river's edge to find that my voice box would hardly operate at all. The cold air made the wet clothing even colder and it was evident that the hunt was at least temporarily off for me.

Just minutes before, I had observed my father reaching down to grasp single handfuls of fine sand and scatter it evenly over the ice-covered rocks. Not only did I wish I had chosen the same route that he had chosen, but needless to say I certainly wished that I had scattered the sand also. He had made it across safely and when I finally gained enough courage to look his way, I saw him nodding his head from side to side as to show his emotions of my early morning disaster.

At least he had retrieved the two dogs I was leading and quickly dealt with the situation at hand. "Go back as fast as you can," he said. "Get to the truck as quickly as possible and go home for dry clothes." I couldn't argue for I was surely miserable and my body seemed to be getting colder as the seconds went slowly by.

I wasted no more time and the Big Rock House Trail was much longer on my way back than it had earlier been. I thought I would never make it, but the pickup truck finally came into sight. The heater was still somewhat warm and I felt lucky to have only endured the serious condition for a minimal time.

Chick had been made aware of the incident by radio and walked briskly to the truck's side. He was always good for a humorous statement or two but didn't seem to find anything funny about what had just transpired. "Sit still until you warm up," he said. He also followed by instructing me not to drive before I was physically competent to do so.

On my way home, I couldn't help but ask myself a long-lined question if the sport I had chosen was hardly worth it or not. Hours of hard work and preparation for such a sport adds up to a horrendous total with a significant price tag added as well, especially on a day such as the one I had been misfortunate enough to be a part of already. It's easy to get discouraged I suppose, when ending up on the short end of the stick in such circumstances. Nevertheless, after positioning my body inside dry clothes at home, I realized again that the rewards of such a sport as hunting with dogs far outweighed a few hours of trial and error.

I was glad beyond a high degree that my mother wasn't there. The house was quiet and I remember discussing with myself how lucky I was to have missed out on both her teasing and complaining. I knew she would have been much concerned about my falling into the cold river but she would have had much of a laugh with it too.

In a matter of minutes, I was back behind the steering wheel and traveling south again on Highway 215 toward Lake Logan. The further I went the more I wondered what was going on with the hunt. I really hated that the morning's unexpected problems had occurred and had to make myself aware of the speed limit over and over on my way back.

On the way, I thought about Henry and how his care and compassion for me was suddenly more important than the hunt. I thought about him not wanting me to leave until he was sure that I was physically able to drive. It made me ask myself if my care for other people was nearly as strong as what he had demonstrated just minutes before. It was then and there at that very second, that I realized the genuine love that Chick had in his heart for each and every one of us as a group.

He lived, ate, and breathed our sport that had been handed down by the generations before us, yet he had a stronger power from deep inside himself. Just knowing that his care for my well being far outweighed anything else that cold morning meant a great deal to me. Those thoughts made me feel better instantly as I drove the last few miles back up the mountainside.

Rounding the sharp right curve at the mouth of Big Rock House Cove, I saw no one there. I stopped for a few seconds to listen from the truck's window and couldn't hear anything but the distant river roar. That was relatively good news though for I then knew that my fellow hunters were on to something and quickly made my way on up the scenic highway.

Little Rock House Cove, which is the next so-called cove to the left side of the Pigeon River was quiet and empty from the party also. I was puzzled as to where everyone had gone in such a short time and kept on driving up the road in the dark so to speak.

Chick wouldn't answer the radio calls that I was so freely transmitting either which made me double worried. "Where could they have gone?" I kept asking myself. The party had to be in the Little East Fork area or higher up Highway 215 one or the other and my patience starting getting harder and harder to find. I couldn't make any sense out of this so far crazy day and simply drove further up the highway toward the next cove to the left called Wash Hollow.

Bright sunshine beamed across its wide mouthed bottom by then and the ice-covered rocks on the side of the road banks glistened the scene. In the midst of my wondering thoughts, and bringing the vehicle out of a sharp right curve not expecting to see anybody, Chick appeared in my line of sight. He was standing on the opposite side of the road and was looking into Wash Hollow. When he heard the sounds of the truck he quickly motioned me to the wide shoulder and turned his head back and forth as to let me know to stop the engine noise as fast as possible. After that signal, he then pointed across the river to make me aware that the pack was there.

The dogs were relatively close too because when I cracked the driver's-side door to a slightly open position, I heard them well and they sounded to be giving tree barks. The best that I could judge their distance seemed to be about four hundred yards up from the river's edge. Chick wasted no time explaining how good the race had been.

Seen here is majestical ice-covered rocks during the winter months in Western North Carolina caused by repeated days of cold temperatures.

At a low whisper, I asked him if any of the hunters were close to the stopped pack and was overjoyed when he told me that Dad was. I wanted to go but Henry assured me that my father would be to them soon so I stood anxiously on the road's edge with him to listen closely at what the next few minutes would behold.

Sounds of another vehicle alerted me and I looked over my shoulder to see it pull onto the grassy side of the highway. Stepping out of it was a man whom I've yet to speak of until now. He didn't speak as to keep a quiet profile and we all stood together by the shiny guardrail listening to the aggressive noises from the dogs.

The good friend that joined Chick and me that day was Tom Plemmons. Tom is a modest quiet-type of fellow and has been a part of many hunting days in the woods with my family. He is of average size and has been a blue-jean man as long as I've known him. He's a lot like my cousin Sheridan when it comes to joking and kidding but all in all, he is as good as they come for a friend.

Tom never seems to get shaken up over anything. Time after time, when certain situations have become quite complicated, I've watched him keep his cool and stay calm and collected much like he was doing that chilly morning. He just stood by the road's edge waiting patiently for some act or the other to break the curiosity while Chick and I paced a hole in the earth from pure anxiety. Tom only watched and smiled.

Finally it happened. The rifle blasts seemed to echo for several seconds and the dogs became quiet as usual. Suddenly they started barking again with some most serious tones and started moving again at a medium to fast pace toward a ridge that separates Wash Hollow from the next so-called cove beyond it named Devil's Canyon.

This ridge is known as Fire Scald. Fire Scald is one of the most beautiful places in the Shining Rock Wilderness. I've been on it many times and have admired its wide open, grassy flats as they so eloquently lay under the large oak trees there on each occasion.

The fading pack crossed the pretty ridge in a zip and was out of our hearing toward Devil's Canyon in near seconds. As we traveled hurriedly up Highway 215, we received a message from my dad on the CB to make us aware of what had gone sour.

His run-together words were of a most mangled assortment as he tried to explain what had transpired in the heat of the moment. Big was his most-used adjective and that the monster wasn't up a tree but was on the ground level with the pack when his face-to-face duel had occurred. He also told us that he was sure of at least one shot out of the three that he had taken at the moving target and would be off of the air until a later time.

Adrenaline flowed with forceful rages throughout our veins as Chick and I rode further up the highway to position ourselves to hear better. I remember Chick saying that it must be a bad one to have escaped my father's presence. "He's one of the finest hands at the final moment that I've ever known," he said and the higher we elevated the mountain the more puzzled we became.

In addition to all of the confusion, toward the end of my father's radio conversation he had entered more figures into an already complex problem. He told us that he had made a mistake before leaving home that morning and had no more ammunition. Henry and I were shocked by the statement and thought silently trying to consider not just one problem, but several. Chick finally spoke up more or less to himself I suppose and shouted that Mackey was with him.

We could only hope that Mackey had some 30-30 shells mixed with his .444s when suddenly my dad came back over the air to make us aware that he had found Mackey again and had borrowed several live rounds from him.

Tom Plemmons, always good for a joking remark assisted by a top-quality personality.

At least that hurdle had been jumped successfully and Chick and I periodically stopped along the scenic highway to listen for the pack. At last we did hear their distant echoes but the steep contour of the surrounding ridges made them bounce from one to the other. After a few moments of speculations, we decided that the sounds were coming from deep within the sharply angled cove ahead.

The dogs had made their way across Devil's Canyon and onto the butt of Buck's Ridge that divides it from the Sixteen Canyon Cove of the Sam's Knob or Black Balsam area. It is virtually impossible to end a bear hunt with any sort of victory when hounds run their prey onto the jagged terrain that is found there. This conclusion is firmly supported by the result of vast rock cliffs combined with heavy brush or filth brush as we know it making for an almost definite escape for bears being chased with dogs.

Many acres of land that lay inside the Shining Rock Wilderness are densely congested with Mountain Laurel and Ivy bushes but none can compare with that of the Sam's Knob portion of the Sherwood Forest. It simply tops them all and knowing that made me overly concerned about how that particular day was to end.

There is a railroad grade of long ago that enters the lower lobe of Sixteen Canyon Cove from Highway 215 and is still relatively open for walking as far as obstructions are concerned. That was my projected path and I was gone as soon as Chick stopped the vehicle.

As I pen these words, I am thankful to my maker for another opportunity to have walked the old railroad grade on this certain day doing the same as I was then, trying to hear the sounds of a distant pack. The railroad grade would arouse most folk's curiosity I suppose or at least it does mine, to think about its use of many decades ago.

Transporting logs was the foremost reason for its existence and imaging the old train cars there puts quite a twitch in my imagination. The grade was built with picks, shovels, and horse-drawn drag pans and there can be no doubt of how the laboring men of that day felt when a day's work was finally completed there.

I ran the grade with everything in me and after climbing over the eighty-foot rock rise at its end, I luckily heard the hounds. To my surprise they were stopped again and wild thoughts raged through my mind if only for one more time. I knew my dad had to be close so I moved with near complete quietness as to not give the monster any reason to leave.

Tom was with me all of the way. Even though our excitement levels were blown out of proportion, we made it a point not to speak to each other at all. We walked the rocks of the Devil's Canyon creek bank so our feet couldn't cause any unwanted noise in the crunchy, frozen leaves. It quickly came time to depart from the creek bed though and start our ascent up the brushy little ridge toward the yelps of the pack.

I wondered again where my father was and suddenly found out. His scarred and battered old Winchester started again. Not once, not twice, but three times and at that point I was only a bundle of nerves. The only consolation I could muster was realizing that the dogs had at least gotten quiet.

I left the creek at an exploding run and didn't slow up until the white color on the dogs caught my eye in the short distance ahead. As I pulled the last two hundred feet in elevation with both hands alternating from one knee to the other, I couldn't believe what my eyes beheld. I immediately realized what my father's descriptive words had meant earlier.

The old railroad grade to Sixteen Canyon seen here gives the steeply graded mountainside an uncommon twist of character.

I had never seen my father as shaken as he was that day. He had taken one of the biggest and most furious black bears in the Western North Carolina Mountains and I was as proud of him as could be. I was astonished at its size and quite simply stood in awe.

Sailor quickly made me aware of his presence too and that finished my day off for the good. He seemed to act as if he was young again and barked excessively at the huge carcass with all of his might. I hugged the old rascal and stroked his short hair vigorously. I was so touched by his actions that I could no longer speak. Those few minutes that followed will never leave me as long as I'm of a sound mind. At that point, there was no doubt of his retirement. He ended his career on a very high note and that is the kind of creature he was and that's the way I wish to remember him.

Getting the trophy out of the woods was much of a task but finally we made it after the sixth hour. I can't say that Chick had waited patiently but he welcomed us excitedly as we arrived at last. I remember him saying over and over that he had never seen a black bear of such a caliber taken in the wild.

We sat there on the shoulder of the road for at least an hour enjoying Chick's marvels and reminiscing the day's excursion together as we rested. We were exhausted but hadn't really taken time to realize it. We were more like a family by then instead of a hunting party and I thought about the many building blocks it had taken to erect such fine relationships as friends.

It was late in the afternoon when we arrived at Henry's house and found all of the women folk there waiting to see the trophy. I wasn't sure how the news had traveled so fast but it didn't really matter. They were astonished at the bear's size along with its beautiful shining coat.

The sun had peacefully ceased behind the western horizon by the time everyone had gotten sufficient looks and the hunting club decided to wait until early morning to take care of the carcass being as we were all exhausted anyway. The cold temperature was sure to preserve it and nothing would be lost to wait.

I remember one of our good friends and hunting partners, Richard Jones, adding a few spikes of humor to the conversation about the huge carcass. He claimed it really didn't matter because there was none of us with enough energy left to take care of anything until the next morning. We all had a laugh from Richard that day as he passed through to view the trophy that my father had so strategically taken.

As I made my way toward Chick's driveway, I placed my arm across his shoulder and he did the same to me. "Well Henry," I said, "we brought this season to an end with a bang and I've enjoyed every day of it too." His eyes watered softly and his lower lip jerked slowly and he hesitated for a second or two. "I think a lot of you boys," he said.

Keeping a somewhat normal composure was all that I could do after hearing that statement from Henry. Little did I know that he had seen the regular bear season close for his last time on earth. We held to each other tightly and nothing else mattered at that point nor did anything else need to be said. Chick had filled the empty space that my deceased Grandpa had left in my heart and at that age of my young life--he was nothing short of a miracle.

SWEPT AWAY

There was no doubt that autumn had expired and winter had begun. The cold drizzle of rain felt as if it was dripping from icicles and I was surprised that it wasn't falling in some sort of frozen form as I looked through the one-inch cracks of the big barn's siding boards. The light hurt my eyes because I had been inside the dark barn since early morning.

Classing Burley tobacco was the project at hand for the bigger part of the next two weeks. The bright leaves hung straight down from the dead tobacco stalks that had been speared two months before on slender wooden sticks. The sticks were suspended off of small birch trees called tier poles that were strung from one end of the barn to the other.

The leaves had become dampened by the high humidity level in the air. When this level of dampness was at the best-suited stage, our family worked diligently to remove the tobacco from the sticks and pull the leaves off of the stalks at a near non-stop pace. This natural dampening process is known as being in case.

Each leaf was pulled off one at a time and laid on what was called a classing board. The leaves on the bottom of the stalk were called the lugs while the ones in the middle were known as the reds, leaving only the ones at the bud end of the stalk called the tips.

I've spent many days in the cold damp barn pulling the tobacco leaves off and putting them in their proper classifications. When the classing boards became full the leaves were picked up in small bundles and tied together with a single leaf. These small bundles were called hands.

Pictured here is some Burley tobacco after it had been speared onto a slender stick and placed on tier poles to cure.

The hands were then placed on a woven wood basket evenly in circular form repeatedly until the basket was about chest high. It was then capped with another woven basket and the two were tied together with a small caliber string making a finished product that was ready to ride to the market for sale.

I understand that Burley tobacco is baled now instead of tied into hands but nevertheless, growing tobacco brings with it a somewhat long and drawn-out process from the time the small seeds are sown until it reaches the woven basket. By the time a Burley tobacco seedling reaches the slender tier poles in early autumn it has been handled approximately six times which made me wonder on many occasions what a man's time was worth.

I can remember as if it were only yesterday what huge piles of tobacco hands we would congregate at the end of an average day of classing and tying. Packing it on the wood slatted baskets was the last thing that was done late in the evening hours. My father and I most always took care of that chore ourselves after whatever other help had gone. Sometimes we would work late into the night hours and though those times alone with him didn't mean a lot to me then--they certainly do now.

This particular day had found us finished just before dark and we walked side by side from the barn toward the house. He mentioned that the wet weather was supposed to continue according to the forecast and advised that we eat a good meal and turn in early to assure our strength for another long day in the barn.

Eventually we did finish on time every year even though we had doubted it on many occasions. It was a happy time when the tobacco work was over and my brother and I looked forward to the trip to the market. Every year, it simply astonished us to enter the huge tobacco warehouse and gaze down the long aisles of full baskets. We usually stood in awe calculating how many man-hours were invested in getting that much tobacco under one large roof.

The beef stew and home-style trimmings tasted exceptionally good after spending the cold day in the big tobacco barn. My mom had a way of cooking unlike any other person I have ever known but then again, I suppose most every country boy would feel the same concerning their mom's cooking.

Following the main course, she never failed to present some sort of dessert and it mattered not what it was-- we could count on it being delicious. This certain night found us having a hard time choosing which pastry or pie to sample for there were several choices. She always had an over abundance of the sweet stuff when December drifted beyond its halfway point.

The Christmas Holidays were upon us and that was forever good news in my brother's and my young lives. Christmas was a special time at our house and we looked forward to the family being together. Listening carefully to each member's big story of the year was good entertainment to say the least.

I was still privileged at the time to have one living grandmother and grandfather. Spending time with them during the Christmas Holidays was grand to me as their memories still are also. They seemed to constantly contradict each other's opinions knowing all along that they would be in somewhat of an agreement when it came to the bottom line. They grumped back and forth as most folk would be expected to do at their age but they loved each other immensely and never failed to live a righteous life making them perfect examples for young lives to follow.

Their names were Claude and Elsie Kuykendall. They resided in or near the Dix Creek community for most of their lives and have been well respected by their friends and neighbors down through the years. My grandfather Claude worked in the nearby small town of Canton as a radiator repairman for close to fifty years while my grandmother Elsie was a homemaker accompanied with many more responsibilities there.

God blessed them with two healthy and active daughters and one son that was plagued from birth with cerebral palsy. This occurrence hampered my grandparent's day-to-day lives and were dictated by it, but together they provided the best possible for him and never gave up on the constant battle of his care.

His name was Bruce. He loved all of us kids and was of sound mind if only his body could have performed properly with it. When he ate, he was fed. When he moved, he was carried. When he talked, he talked with his eyes and watching him communicate silently with his parents was simply outstanding.

They never lost their patience with him though the road became very rocky at times I'm sure. The responsibilities that faced them were long trying ones but they were always happy as they cared for him constantly.

At the age of thirty-six, Bruce became ill and after a four-month struggle to overcome it, he passed. My grandparents were devastated beyond any stretch of thinking as could be reckoned—especially my grandmother. All of us received a strong blow from his death but she responded to the trauma the worst by far. She had been so close to him and had spent every day of the thirty-six years with him.

Claude and Elsie Kuykendall, devoted parents

Bruce, a person to learn from

Grandma Elsie was never the same after Bruce's death and it was evident why. It was quite simple to understand. We as a family coped with the fact for her remaining time on this earth and didn't question it. Even after several years had gone by, she could hardly converse at all unless Bruce was mentioned. She cried often especially during holidays but managed to push ahead with life and enjoyed bits and pieces as she went along.

I thought about my grandparents that night as I ate dessert. Their pictures were on a table in plain sight and the memories of my Uncle Bruce ran vividly through my mind. I was tired from the hard day's work in the barn but thinking about Bruce's lame legs made me reach deep inside myself and muster plenty of excess energy while being thankful to an unknown degree for good health and strength.

The clock alarmed at what seemed to be an unforgiving hour but I finally pulled my body out of the warmly quilted bed and got dressed. I looked forward to the day's work that lay ahead in the tobacco and it wasn't until much later in life that I realized how blessed I was to have felt that way.

I've met many people that have lived their lives as a constant dread. Some dread their jobs while others dread small chores and some even dread to go home in the evening hours. I can honestly state that I have never dreaded a day's work no matter how hard it was to be. I'm also thankful to have certainly looked forward to going home at the end of the workday since I was old enough to do so.

The fire felt good as its heat reflected off of the rock hearth and the smell of another country breakfast filled the air. Waiting on the meal to be completed had a sneaky way of bringing out the impatient part in a young man. At last we did eat and sat talkatively together after the meal to sip down a last cup of coffee. Then we were off to the barn again knowing that we wouldn't be back until dark.

Several days later, the tobacco crop of that year was finally history. The full baskets of tobacco had been delivered to the market, the small wooden sticks had been bundled and the barren stalks had been scattered on the nearby fields to be plowed under as organic matter for the next crop.

The bear-hunting season had opened again after a three-week break for a brief period but we didn't expect it to be nearly as rewarding as the first and regular season. It has proved itself through past history to be somewhat non-productive. Due to that, we only went hunting on an average of two or three times during that short season of the year.

By that time, the weather usually had started to take a turn for the worse which meant that a large percentage of bears would take a den for hibernation thus making most hunting days long and weary ones. Sometimes our party would walk for hours upon hours during the last days of December while leading the hounds and never find a runnable scent from early morning until late in the afternoon.

We had gone hunting once before Christmas and one time afterwards during the short season but hadn't had any luck in finding a bear. Nevertheless, we gathered as a group in the basement of the big log home on Sunday afternoon and made our plans for the final hunt.

New Year's Day marked the complete closing of the 1983 bear season and that meant that the hounds could no longer be loosed on U.S. Forest Service or North Carolina Wildlife properties until the fall of 1984. That was a sad fact that none of us wanted to think about but we all subconsciously knew that our time was quickly coming to a close.

Chick was chipper as usual when we met him before daybreak on New Year's Day. Nothing would do him until he had checked all of our belts thoroughly to see if the Christmas goodies had caused us to back them off a hole or two. I can still hear him as he kidded us young lads about becoming soft over the holidays.

Chick was only joking about the matter but my father was serious when the subject was discussed further. He claimed that a man desperately needed a long hard mountainside climb after junk eating as he called it for several weeks. He referred to it as cleaning the arteries out and according to the projected path that he had laid out for us on the evening before, we knew he meant to do just that.

The slow rain that had fallen on and off for the past three days was sure to have been in some sort of frozen form at the extreme elevations of Cold Mountain. I hoped that it had been snow instead of ice because while walking in snow was to be difficult, the ice would have been by far the worst. Expecting whatever, I was looking forward to spending the last adventurous day with the dogs.

We walked the Brushy Ridge Trail that morning and made our way to the Cold Mountain Swag in close to record time. The air was cold as it entered and exited our lungs and body over-heating was no problem. We enjoyed the walk with the hounds and were just happy to be together again.

The Swag was most beautiful that brisk morning. To our surprise, the precipitation that had fallen only days before in the valley below had fallen at the higher elevations as rain also. Although the leaves were only wet, the near freezing water had transformed into ice on every structure that was above ground level. The weeds, briars, tree limbs and small twigs had a thick one-half inch coating of the clear substance stuck to them. Everything sparkled like diamonds from it and I remember thinking of how blessed we were to have witnessed such a sight.

Several times in my life while roaming and hunting in the woods, I've strangely been made aware of God's astonishing work of creating the little things in life or should I say the only things in life. Standing with the group while amazed at the unique scene before us, I thought about the wealth that each of us gained that morning without the jingle.

None of us had many riches to speak of as far as material things were concerned and I doubt that all of us together would have had enough money in our pockets to have paid for a decent camera in which to snap a picture of the awesome sight. But as we admired it, we held the whole world in our rough chapped hands. I believe every person there that morning truly realized the difference between the wealth that creation has to give and the come-and-go, save-and-spend riches of today's society.

I noticed every member of our group looking over their shoulders as we climbed the trail toward the highest peak of Cold Mountain to get one last glimpse of the majestic scene. The sun had raised higher in the eastern sky making the thousands of ice particles glisten even more.

We short cut the high top trail of Cold Mountain and routed ourselves by the plane crash sight as we so usually did. By entering the north- side slopes, we noticed that the ground was frozen to the extent, which made keeping our feet under us quite difficult for more than fifty feet at a time. The moss that covered the big gray rocks was stiff like hundreds of small strands of wire and it made crackling noises from the weight of our bodies.

Seeing the pieces of metal from the crash scattered throughout the dark gloomy hollow there brought a familiar feeling to my stomach as it always does after noticing it in different places below me. Every time I pass by it, I get that feeling and can't help but dwell for several minutes on the thought of the lives that were lost there on that foggy night in 1946.

As I looked down on the crash sight that day, I tried to imagine what the aircraft crew might have conversed in the few seconds remaining after hearing the whistling propellers start to cut the timber's foliage like some sort of large saw blades. A split second or two was all they could surely have had before the explosion and the thought of it still adds even more gulf to an already eerie feeling each time I visit it.

Before long, we had reached the Old Bald Rocks and still hadn't found any evidence that would lead to a turn loose of the hounds. I had only hunted once in such an unexpected manner in which my father again introduced to us without any warning. "Turn a couple of them loose," he said. Then he instructed us to start unsnapping the pack two at a time at approximately five-minute intervals.

Turning the dogs loose with no track in front of them was still more than risky to my opinion and my dad discovered from the expression on my face that I was somewhat confused again. "Don't worry, they'll be all right," he said. "The pack is made now and they know what they're doing." He followed by advising us to have faith in them. "We trained them right didn't we," he said.

At last, we sat down on the rocks of Old Bald and were glad to do so. All of the dogs were out of sight and as we waited for them to create some action, we spruced ourselves up a bit by consuming a few snacks. It felt good to sit in the sunlight there even though the rocks were cold and clammy feeling under us.

My father suddenly started reminiscing to us about the yesteryears of long ago while spending time with his father in the exact location we were at. He explained how they sometimes hunted the bear dogs without tying them after they had been fine-tuned as he described it. He told several stories in a row and his words seemed to roll naturally out of his mouth as if the information thereof wasn't coming from the mind but from the heart.

He kept one tone of voice as he unfolded several different experiences on or close to Old Bald with his father and though he meant for us to hear every word he didn't want to look us in the eye.

I felt sorry for my dad that day. He missed the man who had started him and trained him in the sport that he so dearly loved. How awful it must have felt to relive memories of a person that could no longer be affected by an adventurous trip to the mountains with him and the hounds. All at once he stopped talking and there was silence throughout. Not even a dog was barking anywhere in hearing distance and it was a solemn time.

The subject was finally changed but was done so by him only. No one had spoken a word for we meant to give him all of the honor that our beings could produce. A few minutes went by and we remained silent. The only way that any of us would have spoken was if we had been asked some sort of question from him. Unknowingly, my dad had a need to call back the image of his father that morning and we wished to do nothing to interfere with that.

"Men," he said, "Do any of you hear the dogs?" I was relieved for the chance to turn my head toward the deep canyons that laid behind us to listen because I was beginning to show some emotion myself. It bothered me to see my father saddened by such a stretch of troublesome sores. He was always a happy man for the most part and I was subconsciously confident that he would overcome it in a matter of minutes.

Dad then attempted to explain some important tips to us as we sat on the rocks of Old Bald that have been precious hand-me downs through the past years. Hearing dogs from Old Bald can be a tricky proposition. Dad made the group aware of the different strategies he had previously explained to me just weeks before that could be successfully sustained from there.

Some of the short cuts and smarter ways to maneuver can only be learned from the experience of a young hunter himself but many corners were cut for us that day as we listened to his valuable advice. We were most thankful for the fine information and glad that Dad had so freely given it to us.

Suddenly, two of the dogs started barking with relatively promising yelps below us in the upper top portion of a particular cove known as Anderson Creek. Anderson Creek has been described to a fair degree in a previous chapter. It contains several small coves in itself that are hidden from most viewing areas.

Anderson Creek is a beautiful north-side cove of Cold Mountain and even though few people know, it is a quite sizable one also. Anderson Creek is the headwaters for the Burnette Cove area, which is one of the chief contributing tributaries to the Big East Fork of the Pigeon River.

The dogs exited Anderson Creek in what seemed only seconds and entered into the left fork of Lenior Creek. As they crossed the dividing ridge, several other dogs joined them and another fine race was on in a matter of minutes. They quickly became louder and louder and contrary to what the near future held in store for us, I reckoned from their complex sound that the hunting day was to be short lived.

The pack stopped near the water's edge in the left fork of Lenior Creek just as I figured them to do. They seemed to be treed as far as I could tell. My dad looked at me with a surprising grin and nodded his head for me to go. No persuading was necessary from him either for the excitement had me ready and I left immediately.

The Mountain Ivy under Old Bald on the Lenior Creek side is as thick as it comes compared to that of anywhere on Cold Mountain but that was nothing new to me. I slithered through it as fast as possible and positioned myself close to the pack within fifteen minutes of my departure.

I slipped as quietly as possible and crawled within thirty or forty feet of the raging hounds to find them looking toward the ground instead of up a tree. I doubted the species of their prey at that point as I remembered the strange method in which we had turned them loose. However, I eased my way further with my prepared Winchester.

The Laurel and Ivy seemed to explode just as I gained eye contact with the bruin. It turned the opposite direction from me and commenced up the steep grade toward Old Bald in a matter of a few seconds. The bear had sensed my presence and refused me the chance of even a running shot.

I was disheartened and dismayed in one sense but happy go lucky in another. At least I then knew that the pack was running a bear and I felt relieved by knowing they had found it on their own thus bringing the race into being by themselves. I was proud of them all and was determined to follow them no matter what the cost.

The slanted inclination back to Old Bald was quite depressing to say the least but I trudged onward. It amazed me how the fifteen-minute downhill jaunt had turned into a struggling forty-five minute drag back up the hill. Though I was winded, I finally made it back to the rocks of Old Bald and after several deep, recovering breaths, I relived the past hour with my father.

We could still hear the dogs but they were deep on the Cold Creek side of Old Bald then and in the heart of even rougher terrain. I was shaking with excitement as I listened to my dad explain how shooting was an impossibility for him too as the dogs passed because of the thick Ivy bushes. They had virtually brought the bear straight to him but there was nothing he could do in the grown-over circumstances there. I remember it being hard for me to believe. We were lucky to have been involved in such an intense race on the very last day of hunting.

The hounds stopped again at the midpoint of Cold Creek. My father and I discussed the situation intensely and after a few minutes of deliberation we decided that I should try again. He was to stay put in case of a repeat but I was confident of the next time around.

My brother had left Old Bald earlier and made his way to a previously mentioned point of the trail known as the Tree Stand. He knew that location stood alone when trying to hear dogs in the right fork and Dry Branch areas of Cold Creek was concerned. A few feet of distance can be the deciding factor of whether or not dogs can be heard in those said places there. I have written before concerning my own description of the Tree Stand. It is of up-most importance to a dog hunter on Cold Mountain but it has little to no physical evidence as to mark itself for a stranger's notice.

The Tree Stand is simply a small oak that measures only ten to twelve inches in diameter. It stands on the breaking point of the Old Bald Ridge overlooking Anderson Creek first and foremost but is located perfectly for cross-wind voices also. Its trunk is worn from years of boot soles skinning up and down it as all of us have climbed it many times to listen.

I felt better knowing that my brother was there for there was no guarantee that the second plan would be successful. Before I knew it, I was off again. I had regained my strength and was thankful for that because there was no doubt of the misery ahead.

The Cold Creek side of Old Bald is as heavily populated with Laurel and Ivy as the Lenior Creek side is but is made worse by the existence of rock cliffs there. Some places on Cold Creek can be downright treacherous not to mention them being quite dangerous.

Anyway, I made the quickest time possible and had a spirit of determination following closely behind me. The minutes went by faster than I had expected and after a hard hour I found myself close to the loud pack again. The jagged rocks and brushy trunks were hard to maneuver in at the bottom of the small ridge where the dogs were sounding off. I looked the small timber with extreme caution and couldn't find any outline of an animal whatsoever above the ground line.

I couldn't believe it had happened again. Getting the slip twice in one day was a little much for a tiring body to endure and I hoped for some sort of a miraculous happening to take place among the overly populated undergrowth. I crawled even further but still couldn't set an eye on the sly creature that the determined pack had bayed.

The dogs sensed that I was close and they starting barking louder and much faster and I was sure that the bear sensed my presence also. I couldn't risk going any closer so I simply waited and tried diligently to sort the white color from the black through the thick brush.

Just as I figured, it happened again. Loud cracks of sticks breaking and small rocks rolling combined with rustling noises of downed leaves suddenly took the floor and the dogs got quiet. The bear had made a break to move and the hounds completely hushed for about thirty seconds. When their barks finally started back I was quickly reminded by the fast pace in which they were leaving that it would be several hard hours before I would see them again if I would see them at all before dark.

It looked to me as if the pack had met up with their match and what a time to have done so. I remember thinking of how maybe we should have just stayed at home that day and I was actually scared for their lives. Without explanation, something from inside convinced me that we were on a bad one and it was worry-some to me as I sat among the thick Ivy bushes alone.

I tried a radio transmission but failed to get a word from anybody and there was nothing left for me to do but start the long incline back toward the Old Bald Trail which was a good half mile away. Subconsciously, I knew that my body was beginning to tire quickly but I started the hard pull with a strong will power to find the pack.

A miserable hour and a half slowly passed before I finally put my feet in the old trail and although my ears were extorted by the driving beats of a pushed heart, I listened carefully for the dogs in every direction. I couldn't hear anything whatsoever and was quite confused.

I tried another radio transmission hurriedly and almost panicked when I noticed that the batteries in the small hand-held device were fading. It was obvious that no one could hear me because of the lack of adequate power although I did make out a scratchy voice vaguely and recognized it to be Chick's. I could barely understand the fuzzy words as they came across the air with a much-needed message for me.

The squelch broke in and out as Henry attempted to explain the most current affair. I managed to hear him say that Dad was with the pack but they were treed in an underground cave on Big Anderson Creek and was involved in a troublesome situation to say the least.

New energy came over me like some sort of spirit when I acknowledged the message from Chick and I changed my direction immediately toward Anderson Creek. Topping a small ridge nearby allowed me the proper altitude as to hear the long laying Anderson Creek area perfectly.

From there, I could only hear one dog barking in the far-off distance. It was then and there that I realized that the rest of the pack was in the underground room with the bear and it frightened me to think of how devastating our New Year's adventure might end.

I covered a lot of ground in little time, putting my body through much misery and exertion. I knew I was late for the occasion and I pushed myself to the extreme through the close-knitted Ivy bushes.

The single dog barks became clearer as I got closer. Finally I arrived to find my father and my brother signaling with their hands against their mouths for me to be as quiet as possible. After checking the scene out, I shrugged my shoulders as to tell them that an explanation wasn't needed because it was evident that we had a problem on our hands that could easily be accompanied with disaster.

My earlier guess proved itself right because all of the dogs were in the hole except for one as I noticed a young lad holding him securely by the collar. I was surprised to see his distorted face and was proud that he had at least seen one of the dogs to safety.

The young fellow was the only other hunter that had joined the three of us that day and there was no mistaking his astonishment caused by the ruckus there. He had suddenly found himself involved in a much-heated situation and was paying close attention to my father's directions because every move seemed to count at that point.

His name is Kenny Banks. Kenny had hunted several times with our family before and seemed to be very interested in the sport of bear hunting. Kenny was and still is a slender sort of guy, built for speed and is also reliable. He and I often look back on that New Year's Day and have had many laughs concerning it but there was no humor to be found at the time of its happening.

Kenny is still a good friend to me and my family and we think much of him. He remains willing to do whatever is asked of him at work or at play and I'll never forget his willingness to do whatever he could to assist us that day in trying to get the dogs out of the ground alive.

Each of us had different ideas to contribute towards their safe recovery. In the midst of discussing them, we luckily noticed several wagging tails appear in the mouth of the hole. On instinct, all four of us grabbed a tail quickly and pulled them out of the hole against their will to safety. We tied them to nearby bushes as fast as possible and felt relieved to have retrieved them.

There were still two dogs in the hole. One of them being the pursuant young strike dog, Timber, and they continued to speak aggressively to their prey. They were out of our sight and we knew there was little time left before they were to be injured severely. We were worried for their lives at that point and strived desperately to think of some miraculous plan.

My brother suddenly spoke of a decision within himself to crawl in the hole with a flashlight in one hand and his trusty Winchester in the other. My dad and I didn't care much for the idea but it was evident that he was determined by it so we upheld his long-shot thought.

"If I tap my boots together, pull me out quickly," he said. I was one stage past nervous as his upper torso darkened into the opening in the ground. Things had quieted exceptionally and for all we knew, the two dogs were finished. To our thinking, they had lost their young lives in spite of it all.

My brother was in up to his belt line and each of us expected some sort of action at any second. Suddenly his body became still and I starred at his feet. To no surprise, his boots clicked together with a fast rhythm. My father and I were already set though and pulled him free of the hole in one jerk.

The two dogs began to bark vigorously again and I remember how happy I was to hear them even though my brother was slightly shaken by the quickened moves inside. I think that all of us were somewhat shocked that the hounds were still alive.

Pictured here is Kenny Banks, an easy-going young man and among the finest for a friend.

The two dogs must have been reminded by my brother's mysterious disappearance that they were out of time also and took us by surprise by simply stepping out of the hole. Joy overtook me as I checked them carefully for more serious wounds and we snapped them to a leather leash.

Nothing more was said after that. The young lad with us didn't have a gun so the three of us knelt close to the hole in circular form expecting the unknown to occur at any second. We waited silently for several minutes but nothing happened.

The birds seemed to stop their chirping. The woods were of total silence. The pack even stopped barking and gave only questionable looks from their faces. There were no sounds to be heard whatsoever. I recall those few moments to have some how cursed us with an uneasy eerie feeling and for the first time in my young life I felt somewhat frightened by what would come about next.

I've never been afraid of any animal or anybody for that matter as long as I could see them and watch their actions carefully. I think that was what had me a bit unnerved for we couldn't see the mad bruin although I knew that it would eventually make a break for the eighteen-inch diameter hole in the ground.

Only seconds later, the three of us heard the thudding pounds of the bear paws coming for the opening and we were aware that a shot must be on the money because their rhythm was that of quarter-note runs.

The time had finally arrived. The first sight of red, fire-filled eyes brought echoing sounds from all three thirty-thirty rifles with it. Dust boiled out of the jagged rock hole and our ears rang from the combined noises.

It was then that the celebration began. My brother and I were overwhelmed by our father's swift shooting abilities and were overjoyed by discussing how he had shot

215

from the hip accurately while we had used the gun sights to be certain.

Young Kenneth couldn't speak at all for several minutes after the ordeal for he was astounded with the situation's ending. He couldn't believe what his eyes had beheld and until this day still talks about the New Year's Day adventure.

The task of recovering the carcass from deep inside the ground was that of a completely different story but we managed to do so and were surprised by its size and beauty. I remember it to be the prettiest one I had ever seen. Its coat was of a wintertime thickness and shined like new coins.

As I recall, my father's walkie-talkie was the only workable one between all of us. Henry answered him immediately when called upon and was overjoyed by the surprise ending. He promised to be waiting patiently on us.

My dad strung all of the dogs up on two or three leashes and led the way in front of the three of us who were dragging the heavy carcass. We rested along the way as usual but stayed on a steady pace down the rocky old path of Anderson Creek.

It was slow and difficult on our tired bodies but we enjoyed every step for it would be late evening at least before the adrenaline levels were to subside. At last we did make it to see Chick absolutely beside himself once again.

It's quite unique to me when I recollect memories of how everything clicked together that particular year. The pack had proved themselves to be true and dedicated along with each club member's trustworthy friendship.

The 1983 season had taught a young man such as myself more than a fair share but the utmost lesson was one in which will stay with me forever. Even though we had started that year with far less than brand name tools, it didn't mean that we couldn't build something to be proud of.

We had first looked at the blueprints of a multi-tangled building that seemed impossible to erect but were willing and committed to give it a try. That willingness enabled us to work our way into something quite extraordinary and I will treasure its memory close to my heart as long as I'm allowed to live.

The end result was a colorful patio offset by an extravagant structure in which we could all be proud of. As a team we had accomplished what seemed to be hopeless and I was simply swept away by it all.

Autumn had left gracefully with winter's extravagance bringing our days of fun to an end. The hunting was over for an extended period but the memories of the fine experiences we had endeavored that year rank highly among those that have not yet been penned as the adventures continue in *Cold Mountain Hunter, Volume II.*